The Road to Hudsar

The Road to Hudsar

Krishna Rajvir

DEV BOOKS

Published by:

DEV BOOKS

2nd Floor, Prakash Deep,
4735/22, Ansari Road,
Darya Ganj,
New Delhi-110002
Phone : 9810236140
e-mail: devbooks@hotmail.com
www.devbooks.co.in

ISBN 10: 81–89835–11–4
ISBN 13: 978-81–89835–11–8
First published 2010

Printed in India

Contents

Chapter 1

KINA LEFT Dalhousie at 8 a.m. to go to Chamba via Khajjiar. The road though narrow and steep, was surrounded by the slopes of mountains on both sides, the high peaks covered by the tall pines, oaks and deodars. The forest was dense and Bhola Ram told her it had rich wildlife. It was dangerous to drive here at night because of the wolves and cheetahs. On the east she could glimpse the snow-clad Dhauladhar Range. A few white clouds floated in the clear sky and the sun's rays bathed the entire valley. Sitting in the back of the car looking around, she was lost in her thoughts.

It was such a happy and carefree life till six months ago, when she was enjoying herself in London. Now there was nothing but problems—not only on the family front, but in her professional and personal life too. If only the world was not so difficult and complicated to live in, the natural beauty all around would have made life so good. She knew Bhola Ram was a good driver, especially on the hilly roads and sitting next to him the young boy, Ramu, kept an eye on him to ensure he did not speed. She started feeling sleepy. It was early October and the winds from the north-west were cold even while the sun bathed the entire valley with its warmth. Inside the car it was warm and cosy.

She did not know when she fell asleep and awoke when the car stopped just as it passed Khajjiar, on the hill overlooking the bridge across the flowing river Ravi and the flattened hill on the other side of the river, on which rested the city of

Chamba with its white palace and green chaugan. During the days of the Royals it was called the state of milk and honey and the English called it the little Scotland of India owing to its scenic beauty.

She recalled having stopped at Sultanpur village, but could not understand why Bhola Ram had stopped the car here. Then she saw her driver talking to a man dressed casually in grey corduroy trousers and a brown tweed jacket. The man was looking at him in anger as he pointed to a deep dent in his jeep. Ramu was watching them. She decided to settle the matter and came out. Coming closer she waited to find out more about the argument and then she heard her driver asking to be pardoned, but the latter was too angry to listen. She went closer and asked 'Bhola Ram what happened?'

'So you're the owner of the car, sleeping comfortably at the back not knowing what your driver is doing!'

She looked at the man, who appeared to be a young officer. She thought it was unfair to blame her, so said, 'May I ask what happened?'

'Madam I was driving and may have dozed off, so I hit this jeep which was standing on the road.'

She looked at the jeep parked by the side of the road. There was a dent on its right door.

'I am sorry,' she said, 'I shall pay for the repairs.'

'How gracious!' The tone was cold as he looked at her.

'Well; what else should I do?'

'Next time, watch your driver and don't sleep while he is driving,' he replied as he got into the driver's seat of the jeep. He was about to drive off, but she went up to him and said, 'You're not only un-gentlemanly, but too rude to talk to. Here I was, being courteous, wishing to apologize and pay for the repair of your damn jeep, but now I am glad it is damaged.'

Turning around, she addressed Bhola Ram, 'Come along. No more apologizing. Let us go, it is getting late.' And without giving a second glance, took the drivers seat and asked her driver to sit at the back. She was very angry. As she started to drive, the jeep overtook her. He honked and stopped a short distance away.

'What a combination! A sleepy driver and now a female; the gender every man should be careful of while driving,' and burst out laughing.

She looked at him with anger, poked her tongue out like a monkey, and drove off at great speed. The man was still laughing and blowing his horn again!

'What a man?' she thought and wished never to see him again.

Kina started driving carefully down the hill and then down the long stretch along the Ravi. It was past 6 p.m. when she reached the old red wooden bridge, which had served this state for centuries. Even though a modern cemented bridge had now been built over the river, the old one was preserved by the rulers as a reminder of the age-old heritage of the state. It was now mainly used by the passers-by to walk across. She drove over the new bridge and was stopped by a policeman at the police chowki at the end of bridge. The policeman looked at a piece of paper he held in his hand and then at the number plate of her car. He asked her for her driving license. She fished it out from her bag. He looked at her and asked, 'Were you driving?'

'Yes!'

'Next time, be careful not to damage someone's vehicle when it is standing on one side of the road!' Kina didn't reply but got angry again. The policeman, looking unimpressed continued, 'It is your first fault here, so no action will be taken against you.'

Then looking at the paper he was holding, he demanded Rs. 200 for damage to the car. The man, whoever he was, was not only rude but conceited, she told the policeman. He ignored her remark. 'What a mean man,' she thought and looked around but could not see any other vehicle. She took out the money and demanded a receipt. She was now visibly furious. She asked the policeman the name of the man but did not receive a reply. She was totally irritated and thought,

'Fancy getting things done through the police,' and decided to teach him a lesson if ever she saw him again.

She thought of her uncle who must be waiting and for her and would be getting a bit worried. This visit to Chamba was after several years and she was excited, but for this silly man, who made her so angry and spoilt her mood. She passed Circuit House, turned left in front of the old post office and drove on past the temple of Hari Har, Radha Krishna, that was centuries old. On she went through the old cemented gate to the road climbing up to the chaugan. It was still maintained for those who wished to climb to the city from the bridge, though it was a steep, stony road.

At the end of the road, on the flat hilltop in a corner at the top of the mound was her grandfather's palatial house. He was a famous contractor and affluent. As she stopped her car at the gate, Kina noted that the house had not changed. It was a two-storeyed brick-cum-wooden house with a green roof and chimneys, surrounded by green woods around the slopes; typical British Architecture. The gates were opened, she drove in and stopped in front of the majestic staircase under the covered porch. The noise made the servant come out and as she left the car, she saw her uncle and aunt when the lights were switched on. As in the past, this house seemed like a jewel shinning in the darkness around. It was so well lit, it reminded her of the golden period it had seen during the time of the Royals. The Royals liked her grandfather Thakur Shamsher Singh very much for his hard work and honesty, and he built the network of state roads, bridges and rest houses, and several official buildings of this state.

'You're late and we were worried. What happened?' her uncle asked.

'Nothing much, just a minor bump with a jeep. But the man was awful. He reported me to police next to the bridge, and demanded Rs. 200 from me through the police.'

'Must be some local!'

'I don't know. He was well dressed, rather young and

seemed to be an officer but driving his jeep without a driver. The policeman refused to divulge his identity.'

'Who could it be?' Both husband and wife looked at each other but then decided to let the matter rest.

They entered the house and she was lost in the past of her early childhood and growing years. Kina went to the bay window of the sitting room and saw the lights all across the valley and mountains, with the sound of the flowing Ravi below. Everything was the same; nothing had changed. At a distance the sound of a flute excited her just as it had during her childhood and she was lost looking at the serenity around this heavenly place. She heard the voice of her aunt, 'Have your bath and then we will have dinner,' and it brought her back to the present. She nodded as she accompanied her aunt to the same room, she always occupied during her frequent visits to this beloved place. Nothing had changed at all, except that the couple had grown older.

Her uncle Thakur Baldev Singh looked so frail she wondered about the future of this place when the next heir, his only son, Thakur Bajinder Singh, would take over, because he lived permanently in America and after marrying Nancy, an American woman, had lost interest in this part of the world.

'What a life,' she thought. She bathed, changed and decided to go to bed immediately after dinner, as she was feeling tired. She recalled her mother's words: 'You're a diamond, but for your fiery temper, and this is not good for your health or for the people around you. Your temper always lands you in trouble. I wonder what will happen to the man who wishes to marry you!' Kina smiled to herself. She knew she always felt tired after losing her temper but at that time, when she was ignited, she never cared about anyone. She recalled the face of the young man and at that moment hated him. How rude to report her to the local police! Mighty man!

It was dawn, and a beautiful morning when Kina opened her eyes. She rose and looked through the bay window at the natural beauty all around, and made up her mind to go out.

In other fifteen minutes she was ready in her faded jeans with a thick polo-neck red sweater, her head covered with a woollen cap and wearing sports shoes. She came down quietly, not wanting to disturb her uncle and aunt. There was dead silence. She opened the main door, went out to the servants' quarter and called out to Ramu. While waiting for him, she decided to go down to the banks of the Ravi and visit the temple of Goddess Sitala next to the wooden bridge. Feeling relaxed and comfortable in her sports shoes, she decided to walk rather than drive.

Together with Ramu, Kina climbed down the old road to the river. There were hardly any people on the road and thought that even here, the hill folks don't like to walk any longer. Though the climb down was easy, Ramu warned her it would be difficult to climb up, but she was determined to walk. They went to the temple on the left of the bridge almost touching the banks of the Ravi. There were quite a few devotees. The temple bells were tolling and the priest was busy with the worshippers. They entered, gave their offerings and respects to the goddess, and received the prashad and a saffron tilak on their foreheads. They crossed the road to the river to touch the cold water and collect some of the white pebbles from the riverbed next to the police post.

She asked Ramu to run and reach the bungalow before the others woke up. Ramu crossed the road and she followed slowly without looking around. The sudden sound of brakes and a car stopping made her run across the road. Something hit her and she fell to the ground. For a moment she didn't know what had happened. Then as she tried to get up she paled when she saw that there was a vehicle very close to her.

Someone shouted, 'Damn you,' and holding her left arm assisted her up.

'What the hell, are you doing at this time of the day, crossing the road without looking? For a moment I thought I had killed you!'

She looked up and seeing the same man she didn't know what to say!

'Oh! So it's you!' A smile covered his face. 'Tell me why are you running around like a wild animal?'

'Please release my arm you're hurting me.'

He immediately released her arm and said, 'It seems the man above,' pointing to the sky, 'is keen to see us together,' and with a sardonic smile, paused and continued, 'I wonder why?'

'Who is the man?'

'The one who does not want you to go up too soon even though you're trying very hard. Yamaraj, Lord of Death,' he said and laughed

'Very funny.'

'It is not Madam, but tell me how long do you plan to stay in this town.'

'Why?'

'It is very important, for I have two option: The first is that I must stay at home, or at least not drive for my own safety. I must be careful with someone who wears the same clothes, it seems like a uniform, the only clothes you wear while roaming around like a wild animal.'

'How rude!'

'Well.'

'It is not an amusing incident,' she said.

'I know. You must be used to it, but for me it is very alarming.'

'Thank you.'

He held her hand and then looked her up and down from head to foot just to annoy her, and with a meaningful smile said, 'Same uniform every time—blue and red. This is the second time you are dressed in the same clothes when you have had a mishap with me. I hope next time, when you try to commit suicide, you wear a different outfit, if you possess one, that is.'

'How rude! You're not only un-gentlemanly but . . .'

'Yes conceited too,' he interrupted.

'Oh so you were at the police chowki!'

'Why not? I had to get my money.'

'Very funny. Release me I must go.'

He bent down, still holding her hand, picked up the three pebbles and turning them over, put them back on her palm. 'Go play with them, but next time don't dare cross the road while I drive or . . . .'

'What will you do?'

'I shall have you kept under police protection for some time.'

'You will?'

'Of course.'

'How dare you!'

'You try it again!'

'I will,' and she stuck her tongue out and ran. She started climbing the steep road to the house and looked back as she heard a horn. She saw him start the jeep, wave and drive off.

'I must stay away from this man,' she thought. 'He is very rude and has no manners. Fancy threatening me with the police,' and then she wondered whether he could be a policeman. Whatever he may be, at that moment she hated him. She looked at the pebbles and recalled his words and in anger threw them down the slope of the banks of the Ravi.

When she decided to drive to Jalakadi to buy Chamba chappals, it was past 11 a.m. However she was stopped on the road in front of Circuit House by a policeman, who told her that it was a one-way road till 5 p.m. As she turned back, she saw a vehicle that was allowed to cross and the policeman even saluted the person sitting in the car. She started arguing with the policeman.

Isn't it wrong to make two laws, one for some and another for ordinary people like me?' Someone called out, 'Kina,' and she looked up. Standing in front of a white ambassador with quite a few men in official suits, she saw her uncle talking to a man standing by the side of the car. She looked at the man in the navy blue suit with his back turned towards her. He was tall and appeared to have some status. She turned her car towards them, this time the policeman didn't stop her and she drove up to where they were talking.

'Wait for me Kina, I will go with you.'

She nodded, but by now the man was talking to another gentleman and her uncle was standing nearby waiting for the man in the blue suit to be free. She thought that he must be a senior officer and looking around observed that there were quite a few people waiting to talk to him.

Her uncle said, 'Sir, meet my niece Kina Kapoor. Kiran, this is Mian Inder Singhji.'

As the man turned, she couldn't speak.

'Kiran?' her uncle said.

'Oh!' she came back to the present and looked at the man, who, with an amusing smile said, 'So you're visiting?'

'Yes.'

Her uncle signalled to her to come out of the car and said, 'She is a surgeon and has come here for a short visit on the way to the Shiva temple at Hudsar, in accordance with the wishes of her mother, my elder sister, to pray and offer what she had promised to Lord Shiva. She is just recovering from a heart attack.'

'Oh. I am sorry to hear that,' he said and as he looked at her with a meaningful smile, their eyes met. She was angry now but he raised his left hand to warn her after looking at her uncle who was busy talking to another officer.

'So you are in this city for short visit?'

'Yes! I hope you are happy.'

'Relieved,' he said, 'the monkey is also a surgeon. . . .' and stopped as her uncle turned towards him and started talking. She looked at the man. He was in his early thirties quite tall, around 5 feet 11inches, and had a fair, lean face with sharp features, large light brown eyes and black curly hair combed back. He was well dressed in a navy blue suit, light blue shirt and red tie. He must be a senior officer she thought. She was so engrossed in her thoughts, that when he spoke and looked up she found that her uncle was nowhere around.

'Kina! What a name! Well it does match an unusual rare species, a bundle of trouble, a monkey, a nuisance and a back-seat driver with a fiery temper, a dreamer and now even a surgeon. Only God can help such a combination to kill not only on the road but even on the operation theatre.' He laughed and continued, 'Now don't stick out your tongue, your uncle is approaching.'

'Oh, I hate you.'

'Good for me.'

He then took a paper from her uncle, shook hands and left without looking at her. Ramu came up to her and gave her a folded paper.

'Who gave this to you?' she whispered.

'The man in the blue suit, he replied. She put it in her pocket and got into her car.

'You were rude Kina.'

She didn't reply. They got home and her aunt said. 'So Mian Sahib is here, we must call him for a meal.'

'You know he has never come, but has never refused either, so I don't think we should.'

'He is here to inspect the deforestation in the area around Chatrari Bharmaur and Hudsar so it will be a long visit. Kina I believe you met him? What did you think of him? Her aunt asked.

Her uncle replied, 'She was a bit rude.'

'I was not.'

'I introduced you and for a while you ignored him, didn't you?'

She decided to keep quiet.

At lunch, her aunt asked her again, 'Kina what did you think of him?'

'Oh he is all right.'

'Now don't tell me that. He is a young, handsome man,' she smiled. Kina nodded.

'Well he is the most suitable bachelor in the eyes of the young women in our state. So many rich and royal families are after him but this young man loves his independence. He is from the royal family of Bharatpur near Rampur Bushaher. He is a very good tennis player, horse rider and polo player, besides being a ladies man. His women are mostly from royal families, but no one knows how many there are, but we know of one now,' her aunt continued, as she winked at her husband.

All Royals are good at sports but her uncle had said that he excelled in them. She wondered why they spoke so much about him but decided not to comment. Her uncle said, 'Kina relax for a while. We will take you to Chamba Club at 5.30 p.m.'

'Oh, no Uncle, I rather go with Ramu to the local bazaar and then to the chaugan.'

'Now don't be so boyish, a free bird, at times it is good to attend social get-togethers also,' and touching her shoulder left.

Her aunt added, 'And please put these jeans and sweater into the box. Ever since you have come you have worn the same clothes!'

She went to her room and as she lay down, she remembered the paper given to her by the man. She took it out and read it: 'No change in uniform. Poor girl but with such a fiery temper. You owe me Rs. 300 more. If you don't give it to me I shall get it through a police chowki. Inder.'

'Oh how I hate him!' Although he was a Royal, what a miser he was; demanding more money and threatening to get it though a policeman. He was rude too, to comment on her outfit and looking at her from head to toe repeatedly, just to embarrass her. As her thoughts wandered over these incidents, she fell asleep.

Chapter 2

At about 6 p.m., they drove to Chamba Club, near Circuit House, where the chaugan started. She was a reluctant guest but had no choice because her uncle and aunt were regular visitors there.

'You should be more social,' they both said, and she nodded to please them. She felt irritated that they were behaving so much like her mother. As the car entered the driveway she noticed that nothing had changed. The beautiful palatial building, though renovated, still had the old English architecture with the same green tin roof and chimneys, and was well maintained. The car park was full, and it appeared to be the most sought after place by the officers and noted families of the city. During the time of the royals, it was only reserved for them, their senior courtiers and the British Resident and his officers.

She entered the hall which was fully lit, with several people dressed in their best evening attire. No wonder her aunt insisted she wear a formal dress. So she wore her black wool Kullu dress, comprising of a loose kurta with fine embroidery, tight pyjama trousers, a matching scarf and a pashmina shawl. The only jewellery she wore, which her aunt insisted on, were small ruby ear studs and a few red glass bangles. She tied her shoulder-length hair tight into a pony tail and wore black high heels. When she came down the stairs, the couple appeared pleased and her uncle said, 'Why don't you always groom yourself like this?'

At the club, her uncle joined the men at the bar, while her aunt went to one of the tables to play cards. She was amused by this segregation of the sexes. A few women were sitting on the sofa sipping tea and gossiping.

'What a bore!' she thought, 'what a waste of time,' but there was no escape. So she sat near her aunt and watched them play. As she looked around, she saw a couple entering the hall. The man in a black suit and a white silk shirt with a matching silk tie of white polka dots on a black background was none than Mian Inder Singh.

'What bad luck,' she thought 'he has to be wherever I am.'

She then looked at the woman. She was tall, reaching his shoulders, with a willowy body, wearing a thin, dark green chiffon sari, with a low-cut choli. Her head was fully covered and she was carrying a deep green pashmina shawl. Her jewellery was heavy with diamonds and emeralds, and appeared expensive, but it suited her. She looked sexy, even though she was covered by the sari.

She appeared to be well known, and everyone stood up to greet her with respect and smiles. As she turned and looked towards the card tables, Kina realized that she must be in her early thirties and was really beautiful. She had a flawless, fair complexion, a lean face with sharp chiselled features, and her big black eyes added to her beauty. Her long, shining, black hair fell down her back and her make-up was perfect, adding even more to her beauty. The couple was definitely the most handsome in the club.

She turned to her aunt, who whispered, 'She is the granddaughter of the royal of this state. Kina nodded and said, 'She is beautiful.'

'Yes, but the same can be said about the man,' her aunt rejoined and smiled at her. Kina was amused, and thought that had her aunt been aware of her encounter with this man, she would not have talked about his good looks.

The girl strolled up to the card table and a woman called

Salochna Devi got up and said, 'Come here your Highness,' and vacated her seat for her.

Her aunt turned to her with a smile and said. 'Welcome to the club, but we are seeing you after a long time Sita Deviji.'

'Yes! I spent a long time at Shimla,' she replied in a husky voice, looking at Kina.

'Oh, meet my niece, Kina, she had just come from Dalhousie for a short visit.' The woman looked at Kina, nodded with a smile, and ignoring her further, picked up the cards and started playing.

'What a royal snob,' Kina thought. She didn't like the cold tea so put it under her aunt's chair. She called the waiter and took a glass of apple juice, drank some and poured the cold tea into it and pushed the glass, now full, under the chair. Then picking up the empty glass she started tapping it with her gold band on her middle right finger. Her aunt frowned and said, 'Kina don't!' She nodded, and placing the glass under the chair turned to watch the card game. Finding it boring, she decided to go to her uncle and looked towards the bar. Mian Inder Singh was holding a glass and looking at her. There eyes met and he smiled and winked.

'He is a teaser,' she thought, 'fancy having such a beautiful girl and then winking at me.' She decided to avoid him. She was getting really bored and felt suffocated. She looked at the roof and then around but didn't know how to escape or pass the time. The only person who could be a help, was her uncle, but she was too scared to look in his direction, because of that man. She decided to go outside, and when she saw a waiter approaching the table, she signalled to him. She asked him about the way out and he pointed to a door. She took out a five-rupee note from her pocket, gave it to him and said, 'Show me.'

He took her to the end of the hall and opened the door for her. She turned back to see her aunt still playing cards, smiled and then looked towards her uncle, but the same man was still looking at her with an amused look. She was angry now, so she poked her tongue out at him and left the hall.

Coming out into the open she saw the vast lawns with chairs scattered around, and though it was cold, the wind refreshed her. Walking slowly, she approached a chair and sat down. A waiter came up to her and asked if she would like some fresh tea, she said, 'Thank you but tell me how I can go up that mound to the temple?'

'There are two paths to the temple. You go out, turn and take the stairs to the temple. There are 108 steps from Jalakadi, and it may be too difficult for you. The other is to drive around the slope of the hill and that would be easier for you,' he replied.

As the bells started tolling in the temple, the waiter said, 'If you wish to go, you must go now, you can't visit the temple at night.'

'Why?'

'No one goes there after the temple is closed. There is danger from the wild animals from the dense forest, and a lion has been seen by many people, that they call Goddess Kali's vehicle.'

'Thank you for telling me all this.' The temple bells were tolling and it tempted her to go up. She decided to get the keys from her uncle but then thought of the man looking at her. She abandoned her wish and decided to go in the morning. Taking out her diary she started writing in it to forget her boredom.

A soft cough brought her to the present. She looked up and the man she least wanted to see was standing behind her.

'So you're here! I noticed your restlessness and boredom. So the Australian lamb in blue jeans has changed to a Kullu lamb. But whatever it is, the change has added some beauty to that ugly face.' He said.

'How dare you talk to me like that!' She said and got up

to leave. He caught her left wrist and said, 'What a temper! One must say it does add charm to your personality,' and then looked her up and down. With a smile, he added, 'Not bad!'

'Oh, what should I do!'

'Nothing.'

'Oh I wish you would leave me alone.'

'Now let's talk sense. You are keen to go to the temple; come I shall take you!'

'Who told you?'

'The waiter whom you gave five rupees to and I gave ten!'

She couldn't stop laughing and said, 'You're the limit!'

'Am I?'

'Yes.'

'Now come!'

'All right, butÖ'

'No buts and don't worry, we will return in a short time and no one will notice!'

'What about your girl?'

'Oh Sita. You're jealous!'

'Why should I be jealous?'

'Then don't worry,' he replied. Holding her wrist, he took her to the other end of the lawn, opened the gate and they walked together to the white ambassador in the car park. They got into the car and drove down the road to the temple without talking. After a while, he asked her, 'Do you write?'

'Yes,' she replied, 'occasionally.'

'What do you write?'

'Poems and thoughts.'

'What a deadly addition to the other combinations.'

'What do you mean?'

'Well while travelling you sleep, a day dreamer, a woman with a fiery temper and now a philosopher. I must stop driving a car while you're in this city to keep myself safe from accidents!'

'Very funny!'

'Don't you think so? I do,' and he laughed.

Now she was relaxed and started enjoying his light-hearted company. He stopped the car by the side of the road and then holding her hand started climbing the small steep path up to the mound and the courtyard of the temple which was fully lit. But the temple was now closed. She paid her respects to the central statue of the stone Bharion, looked up at the temple, closed her eyes and prayed. But then she turned to look at him and blushed, as he was standing near her, looking at her. To overcome her embarrassment, she said, 'Why don't you pray?'

Standing so close to each other, their eyes met and for a while they were lost. Then he returned to the present and said, 'You want me to pray Kina?' And he looked up at the temple closed his eyes and prayed as she watched him.

'Tell me what did you wish from the Goddess?' He asked.

'I prayed to have my mother with me for a longer period,' she said, 'what about you?'

Hc looked at her with a sardonic smile, 'I shall tell you if you promise something.'

'All right.'

'Can we be friends?'

'Yes.'

He held his hand out and she put hers in it. The hand closed and he whispered, 'My friend Kina, won't you say my name?' As she looked at him and their eyes met, she found herself lost in them, but as his grasp tightened, she said, 'Yes, Inder.' And suddenly feeling shy, she turned her head away.

'Well I asked the Goddess to keep the upper storey of this girl standing besides me cool, to save her from a brain haemorrhage,' and laughed!

'You did?'

'Yes, I won't tell a lie in the Goddess' courtyard. Now close your eyes and I shall guide you. Open them only when I tell you. I promise you the best view of this city at night.'

She closed her eyes as he guided her to the edge of the mound and then asked her to open them. Standing at the edge of the mound, she saw the full city lit up in front of her and the scattered lights beyond, on the mountains. To the north-west were the snow-capped peaks of the Dhauladhar Range. She was lost in the beauty of what she beheld and even forgot the man standing besides her. A cough, made her turn, and in her excitement she held his elbow and said, 'What should I say but, thank you.' She smiled up to him, but the smile vanished as their eyes met again.

Holding her to him, he bent down and said, 'I am in a dilemma about what I should or should not do. I can't decide what do about the sudden alteration in my feelings, which are changing so fast in spite of fighting to control them.'

Then holding her close, he placed a soft kiss on her forehead and whispered, 'Let us go, before something happens.' He continued looking deep into her eyes for a while, and then suddenly almost dragged her to the car.

On their return to the club's car park he told her to walk through the back door and enter the hall and he would take the front door. Then with a smile, he held her again for a second and said, 'I don't want you to go.'

'Why?'

'I don't know.'

'Please,' she whispered, still looking into his eyes, and holding on to him, said, 'Good night.'

Her aunt was standing next to her uncle and said, 'Where were you?'

'I went to chaugan.'

'You must have been bored,' her uncle said, hugging her affectionately. 'Now let's go and eat,' he said as he escorted the two women to the table where people were filling their plates. She looked around but he was nowhere to be seen.

'What is wrong with me? Why do I want to see him?' she wondered as she recalled those eyes looking so deeply into hers and how both of them were lost.

Then she saw him enter the hall and approach his girlfriend, Sita Devi, who was talking to an elderly gentleman. He said something to her and turned to leave the hall. Standing near the door, he looked at Kina for a few seconds, smiled and left. She wondered how a simple fight could turn into a friendship and what would happen next.

On the way home her aunt told her that Sita Devi had been after him for a long time, but to date there was no news of their settling down together. Her uncle wondered why Mian Sahib left so suddenly without giving any excuse and returned, only to leave again. 'Even his girl was surprised. He never did such ungentlemanly things. Fancy leaving the girl alone!'

It was late when they returned to the house, so they went to their rooms. As she changed she discovered that her diary was missing. She thought she may have left it in the lawn so called the club, but the waiter said that they couldn't see anything there. As she put her phone down, it rang. She picked it up thinking it must be from Dalhousie, but it was Inder.

'Well just to tell you, your diary is with me! Now don't loose your temper. Just stay calm. Please Kina let Devi fulfil my prayer though it may take some time, but I want my Kina to smile more often now.'

'Please don't readÖ.' The instrument was put down on the other side. Now she was not only angry but restless. This was the small book in which she wrote her thoughts periodically. She was not happy that he would discover her personal thoughts and learn about her personal life. Suddenly she remembered the poem she had composed just before he came to the club lawns and her face turned red.

Dusk all around as the sun sets.
Temple so calm where the Goddess rests
Forest so dense, trees so tall
Valley so green, river so fierce

This land of my birth, I love so deeply
I came to thee to regain my peace.

She lay for some time listening to the flow of the Ravi below. Then the silence reminded her that it was late and as her head touched the pillow she went into a deep sleep.

It was past 8 a.m. when her uncle entered her room and said, 'Do you wish to go to your favourite place Jote?'

'Yes!' She was excited.

'Then get ready. Mian Sahib is coming for coffee on the way to Jote to discuss some problems with me about his orchard. Why don't you go with him? It will be a short trip and while he inspects his property, you can go to our house where you stayed as a child, enjoying the apples and the trekking.'

'Oh! I thought you were going.'

'I would have liked to be with you Kina, but neither of us goes to such heights these days. The doctor has advised against it. You must go. It will be good for you and you will enjoy it. Mian Sahib is a close and good friend of our family since the time his father visited your grandfather and the two families came to know each other. He is coming at 10 a.m., so I shall talk to him now.'

'Please leave it.'

'You can check up on Bahadur also. See whether he is working honestly in our absence or not. That would be a favour for us, Kina,' her uncle insisted. Then he continued with a smile, 'Be careful. Don't be rude like yesterday, or show your temper. Don't get bored with him either. He is a royal, and you know these royals are unpredictable at times.'

Though she was excited at the thought of being with him again, she was also scared of her feelings. This simple friendship was getting serious. In order to tease him, she decided to wear her blue jeans and navy blue polo neck pullover.

She went down to breakfast and pretended to try and

change the couple's minds but her uncle and aunt were determined. Her aunt also told her to change her clothes as she would be travelling with Mian Sahib, who was always so well dressed. She went to her room and changed into her dark grey woollen trouser suit. A knock at the door and the information that he was waiting, made her put on her sports shoes and picking up her woollen cap and muffler, she went down.

As she entered the door of the sitting room she saw her aunt giving him a cup of coffee. She waited and then stepped inside. She placed her bag and other stuff on a chair and turned. Holding his cup, he looked at her closely, from head to toe with a sardonic smile. She blushed and looked at her aunt, who was busy serving her husband. How bold, she thought and turned to him in anger to poke her tongue out, but he winked at her and then warned her by raising his left hand.

Her uncle said, 'You have met Kina my niece, Sir?'

'Oh yes! When she was arguing with a police inspector, and I had to help out.'

'Yes. Kina is always getting into trouble due to her fiery temper, but I love her more than any of my other nephew and nieces.'

'Really why?'

'Because she was so different from the other children. Boyish, casual and careless about her dress; always annoying her mother for being a tomboy, even now, when she has grown up.'

She was now very conscious of his looking at her with a meaningful smile, while sipping his coffee. She refused coffee knowing that she was nervous, and if she were to spill it, he would be amused.

'You were asking me how to tackle the menace of lizards in your farm at Jote and that reminded me of Kina and my nephew Rajan during their growing years. Once a lizard bit Kina while she was eating an apple. So both of them, who were very close to each other, decided to teach the lizard a lesson. They spent hours trying to catch and even kill lizards at with pebbles while sitting on a boulder. Then they got airguns and at the end of the day they would count how many they had killed. My mother used to tell them not to do this, or in their next life the lizards would take revenge on them.'

Inder laughed, 'Yes, they are very revengeful; poor lizards. Do you think Thakur Sahib, that she will solve my problem? But seeing her in a temper, I don't think I can trust her. Who knows, she may even shoot me with the airgun.'

'That is true; which is why I do not recommend her,' her uncle laughed.

Taking a last sip of coffee, he rose and thanked her aunt.

'You must visit us often Sir, this is the first time and we are honoured,' her uncle said.

Inder turned to Kina and said, 'Madam if you're ready, can we leave?'

She nodded and rose, put her arms around her uncle and placed a kiss on his forehead but by chance looked straight and her face turned red. Inder was watching her with a meaningful smile. He spoke to her uncle as they walked to the jeep.

Her uncle looked at the jeep and said, 'So the dent is repaired.'

'Yes! It turned out to be a costly affair.'

'How much?'

'The man charged me Rs. 500, and I am determined to retrieve the money from the owner of the sleepy driver of the car to teach a lesson.'

'You must.'

Then turning to her Inder said, 'Madam please sit down,' and opened the door for her. He shook hands with her uncle and taking the driver's seat blew the horn. The white ambassador followed the jeep with his driver and two guards. She looked at him; he was dressed in deep green corduroy trousers and a dark brown suede jacket. He was a very handsome man, and her aunt was right, he was always well dressed.

'So we are going to Jote, Kina, and that too together.' He smiled at her as he turned towards Circuit House.

Chapter 3

INDER STARTED the car and for a while concentrated on driving. As they came to Circuit House, he slowed down. A police officer saluted him and allowed the car to pass. Kina turned to look at the man in uniform and found Inder smiling.

'Something amusing you?'

'Yes. The incident that made me look at the tomboyish girl in her faded jeans and thick red sweater more closely, yesterday.'

'Very funny!'

'It was, and your uncle seemed alarmed at your outburst of temper.' He took a right turn and said, 'Look at the mound and those stairs, leading to the temple, where the Goddess resides. It is so quiet.'

'Return my diary!'

'Why?'

'It is not nice to steal things.'

'Isn't it Kina? Then what about you?'

'I never steal.'

'You did, and I will tell you soon.' He looked serious and she wondered why.

'Well she blessed both of us last night and brought two warring strangers together, to be close friends. We are, aren't we Kina?'

'Yes.'

'Can't you take my name?' he asked and when she did

not reply, continued, 'Say it right this moment or I shall do something which will create gossip in this small town.'

'You wouldn't dare!'

'Wouldn't I?' and he slowed the car.

'Please Inder we are close friends,'

'That is better,' he said and smiled.

As they drove through the cantonment to the road running along the banks of the Ravi, he pointed to the police check post, laughed and said, 'I shall never forget that evening, but you were so worked up, called me ungentlemanly and a conceited man.' He smiled and continued, 'Well friend, let us enjoy the natural scenic beauty together.'

They drove up the steep climb on the narrow road and for a while he concentrated on driving. They came out on to a straight stretch up on the mound among the paddy fields of Village Sultanpur. The sky was clear and though sunlight bathed the valley, the winds from the north-west were so cold that she closed the window of the jeep.

'Feeling cold? I can't imagine a Pahari maiden feeling cold,' Inder said as he touched her right hand. When they arrived in the middle of the valley he turned and parked his car on the side of the road.

'This is the village of Sultanpur, from here you have the most magnificent view of your beloved birthplace, Chamba. No Kina, no more mention of the diary. It is mine now. I am in no mood to argue. I just want to enjoy my girlfriend.' He laughed, got out of the car and opened the door for her.

He whispered, 'Close your eyes till I tell you to open them.' She obeyed, and blushed violently when he bent down and placed a kiss on her forehead.

'What was that for?' She asked.

'You did the same thing to your uncle, before leaving. Don't open your eyes. That was when our eyes met. What was your reaction Kina? At that moment you seemed rather shy.' 'Why should I tell you?'

'You will, or my official car is now just a short distance away.' Inder said.

'Oh, you! I was reminded of the night you first placed a kiss on my forehead.'

'So you did think of me as I did of you? Tell me.'

'Yes!'

'Now open your eyes.'

She looked at the view, the river, the bridge and then on the mound, the city of Chamba, with hills on both sides, and the two temples. On the left of the palace was the temple of Goddess Kali and to the right, the Sui temple. The wife of Sahil Varman, the founder of this city, sacrificed herself to bring water to the city of Chamba.

'The festival of Sui is held in the first week of August and you will attend it next year. This is my promise to my Kina,' Inder said. 'It is only attended by happily married women.'

Looking at her red face, he laughed and said, 'What a beautiful view.'

Kina turned with a meaningful smile. It vanished as he was looking at her and she was lost in his large, beautiful, brown eyes. A passing vehicle brought them back and he said, 'Look towards the north-west, at those snow-capped peaks of the Dhauladhar Range. She looked at the beautiful sight and was lost in it.

'Now dreamy head let us start or we will return to city beautiful without going to Jote.'

She nodded and with a smile said, 'The palace is so beautiful, don't you think about your gorgeous girlfriend at such a moment?'

'She is gorgeous, Kina.'

'Yes, and just the girl for you.'

'Thank you, but stop matchmaking or I shall kiss you at this very spot.'

'You won't,' and ran to the jeep. He walked slowly, got into the jeep and started it. He then bent and kissed her directly on her lips. He said, 'I wish I was alone with you at this moment.'

He started driving and appeared relaxed, 'Why didn't you stay for dinner last night?'

'I didn't feel like it. I saw you eating while standing in a corner and I had a strong urge to be with you, so I left for our safety. I missed you. I rang your uncle this morning and couldn't refuse the offer for coffee, because I wanted to see you again before leaving for Jote. I was surprised and delighted to receive the request to take this bundle of trouble to Jote with me, to your uncle's farm. But I had to pretend and agree like a gentleman!'

'You did? Like a gentleman?' she looked at him with a meaningful smile and continued, 'I don't trust you when you say you wanted me to come!'

'Don't you?' He looked at her and nodded. 'I did. Very much Kina.'

As he drove up the steep narrow road under the canopy of tall pine trees, she suddenly saw the house with the red roof surrounded with fruit trees in front. She was so excited, she touched his elbow and said, 'Look Inder! That is the house I spent so much time in during my summer vacations.'

He turned and firmly holding her hand replied, 'One of the reasons I fell for you is that you're so different from others who spend long hours trying to woo men. Not now, but very soon, in the near future, I shall tell you something about myself.'

He stopped at the gate of a cottage. A man was waiting to open it and Inder drove up to the porch of a white cottage with a red roof and chimney. He came around to open the door for her and whispered, 'Welcome to my favourite place, Rose Cottage. You're the first person to come here with me Kina.' He raised her face looked deep into her eyes and with a smile gently kissed her lips. The door opened and an old man came out. He bent down touched Inder's feet to pay his respects and then waited.

'Ramu meet Kina my very close friend.'

Holding her hand he led her into a room after crossing the veranda. It was so unlike their house next door, which was larger, but appeared almost bare in comparison to this house. The cottage was smaller, but the entire floor was covered with a thick Persian carpet. The sitting room had wide bay windows and the entrance had thick, red velvet curtains with lace down the centre. They were currently parted and provided a view of a tastefully furnished room with leather sofas and expensive antique pieces on the tables. There was a fire in the gate and the room was warm.

Looking out of the bay windows she saw a green lawn, surrounded by beds of roses of different colours and types. Across the slope, covered with trees, she saw that the house of Gaddi Ghori was still there behind the mountain. For a moment she forgot everything and was lost in the past, but returned to the present when he gave her a glass of apple juice and turned to make his drink.

'Is it necessary to drink Inder?'

'Why?'

'I just asked.'

'Not very! You don't like me to drink?'

She smiled and said, 'I have no right but Ö'

He put the glass on the table and holding her said, 'Tell me.'

'I don't like alcohol!'

He looked at her for some time still holding her and whispered, 'I shall never drink again if you promise me something. Say "I promise Inder".'

She repeated the words.

Lifting her face and looking deep into her eyes, he said, 'You will never end this friendship that has become so very deep, by taking a snap decision on your own. Promise me that you will come to me to tell me the truth, the reason, Kina and at this very moment I will promise that I shall never touch a drink.'

'Yes! I promise.'

'But, this is a decision taken by a royal and you know at times blue blood is unpredictable,' and then bent down to kiss her. The simple kiss became more passionate and as his hold tightened, she put her arms around him and holding him started responding to him. Suddenly he moved his face away and almost pushed her from him. He said in an accusing manner, 'You are making me do this Kina and I feel irresponsible.' He left the sitting room abruptly and she sat there like a statue not knowing what to do. She waited for him, for a while, and then decided to go out.

She knew she had fallen deeply in love. Leaving the cottage, she went down the narrow lane between the well-laid apple trees to the edge of the mound and sat on a boulder looking around. He was nowhere to be seen. She wondered where he could be. Just then she saw a big lizard on the ground and it made her smile. She picked up a pebble and with one eye closed decided to strike it, but failed. This made her stand and try again, and when after a few more attempts she succeeded, she sat down again and smiled. A soft laugh made her turn.

Making place for him to sit she said, 'Come Inder, come and sit. We are close friends.'

As he sat next to her, she looked at him and whispered, 'Everything that happened earlier is, in medical terms, a simple physiological reaction,' and she laughed.

The hand that slapped her left cheek was not light. She touched her cheek and looked at him in astonishment, not knowing what to do.

'So it was a joke for you? A simple physiological reaction?' His voice was cold. There was silence and then he took her in his arms and said, 'Don't ever say that again Kina. It was not a simple reaction. What I said and did was a reaction to something within me, making me serious about you. I don't know if it is love, but it is definitely not infatuation. It is a true feeling for you. You will know very soon what I am talking about, my girl.' He touched her cheek gently and kissed the place where the slap had landed.

Suddenly he asked, 'Are you hungry? Let us eat.'

The dinning room was equally tastefully furnished and the expensive china plates were laid out on the table with silver and gold cutlery and several dishes. She looked through the bay window at the dense forest and said, 'The forest was full of wildlife during my grandparent's days. They would hunt with the British.'

'Did they?'

She turned and suddenly realized that being a royal, he must know more about this and felt foolish. He led her to the table and they started eating, but she found him very quiet. 'Something wrong?'

'No.'

'Why are you so quiet?'

'I am thinking about this sudden change in my life. It has actually happened too fast and I have not had the time to look back and think about it.'

'I am sorry.'

'You should be. You stole what I had.' He laughed and said, 'You know only a week ago, I came here and I was determined to settle down with you know who.'

She smiled and said, 'I know Sita. You must, she will be good for you. She is so beautiful and a royal of your status.'

'Do you really think so?'

'Yes.'

'Look at me Kina and then repeat it.'

He held her hand and as she looked at him she was lost in his eyes.

'Repeat it Kina.'

'I can't.'

'No. You will never be able to say this again, and the same goes for me. I know myself. The situation is no longer in our hands.'

He took a piece of chicken from her plate and said, 'It is as bad for you to eat and get fat as it is for me to drink!'

'I am sorry.'

'You should be sorry for stealing someone's man,' and winked. 'However, as far as drinking is concerned, don't worry. I will keep my promise to my Kina. But then I never felt the same for Sita as I do for you. And that too, it has happened in such a short time. What fate.'

As they finished eating, Ramu entered and said, 'Sahib, the Tehsildar Sahib has come!'

'Oh, I must meet him,' Inder said and left her.

She walked around the cottage and entered the bedroom. There were bay windows all around and the sun bathed the entire room. She lay down to have nap. She was fast asleep, and felt cosy when someone covered her with a warm blanket. Murmuring something, Kina went back to sleep. Her hair being stroked and a kiss on her forehead awakened her. She looked around and saw that there was no sunshine in the room. Inder was sitting close to her watching her. She felt shy and was about to get up, when he stopped her. Stroking her hair gently he said, 'Had a good sleep Kina?'

After a while he said, 'It is time for you to visit your uncle's farm, so get up.'

She went to the bathroom, washed her face and came out to find him staring out of one of the bay windows. As she came up to him, he turned and holding her elbow led her out of the cottage. Together they walked to her uncle's farm. When she saw Bahadur, she forgot everything and ran up to him, gave him a hug and said in Pahari, 'I am so glad to see you.'

'You have not changed, my child Kina,' the old man looked at her with affection, and holding her hands said, 'the same Kina, so kind, has come to meet this old man.'

She smiled and asked him for apricots. He nodded went into the house and brought some for her. She took a few and giving him some money, she turned to Inder who was standing at a distance watching her.

'Let us go you must not be late.' He didn't reply and they walked back to the cottage.

'Let's have tea first, there is time,' Inder said and led her to the sitting room.

Holding her he looked deep into her eyes and spoke in a low voice. 'I don't know what to say, Kina, but watching you with the people associated with your childhood has convinced me that so far I am not wrong about the way I feel for you. Yes I do love you.' He bent down and kissed her.

Shortly after 6 p.m., they started the drive home.

'Did you enjoy the adventure?' Inder asked Kina.

'Yes, except for the slap,' she replied as she touched her left cheek.

'My Kina,' he slowed the car, touched her cheek and said, 'I am not sorry! Never take my true feelings lightly.'

'Yes. I am sorry.'

'You should be.'

'Now I have apologized, so don't keep repeating the same thing.'

'So the temper is back. I must do something to calm you down!'

'That hurts. You're cruel.'

'Less than you. Fancy hurting that poor lizard.' He smiled and continued, 'Your mark with the pebbles with one eyes closed was not bad. I wish I had a camera to catch you in that act.'

'Well what about eating some apricots?' Kina said to change the subject.

'No thank you.'

'They are sweet,' she said, taking a bite on one.

'All right, but you have to put it in my mouth, because I am driving.' She did and waited.

'They are very sweet. Why do you talk in your sleep?'

'I don't.'

'Yes.'

'What did I say?'

'You said,' and giving her a sidelong glance, said, 'Please Inder, I love you. Don't ever leave me.' She blushed and didn't know what to do.

'You are fibbing.'

'Why should I? I was happy that your feelings were out in the open and are the same as mine.' He laughed.

'Now I hate you!'

'But at this moment I do wish to be alone with you and to love you.'

There was silence as he concentrated on the steep, narrow road down the hill. As they approached the bridge, Kina asked him to stay on for dinner. He declined, and when she asked why, he said, 'The old couple, especially your uncle, is a very good judge and he will easily detect the change in us, so I won't stay for dinner, though I love to be with you. You will ring me at 10 p.m.'

'Why?'

'Because I want you to.'

'All right Sir,' she said with a smile.

'I hate this meaningful smile of yours,' and he pulled up the car to one side, held her in his arms and said, 'I shall never leave my Kina who loves me as much as I do.'

They arrived at her uncle's house and as she emerged from the car, Inder said, 'Do ring me at 10 p.m.'

Chapter 4

AT 7 A.M. THE next day, Kina left Chamba with Bhola Ram and Ramu to go to Bharmaur en-route to Hudsar. She was happy that her mother was better. Sitting at the back of the car, she started looking around at the scenic beauty. The chaugan was deserted, with just one or two young men taking their morning walks. The shops were closed, but the bells were tolling in all the temples, reminding her that this was a city of temples.

She recalled her grandmother saying, 'You were born at 4 a.m. and your first cry coincided with the first tolling of the bells at the Lakshmi Narayan Temple.' After that, her grandmother was confident, that their first granddaughter would be lucky not only for herself, but also for her parents and grandparents. They discarded the ritual of celebrating only the birth of male children, and held a big celebration on the birth of their first female grandchild. Everyone believed her grandmother, when three days of snow suddenly stopped after her birth.

She looked at the mound near the Chamba Club where the Goddess Kali resided in her temple. She recalled her first encounter with Inder and blushed. She was at the temple of Sui and recalled how he said that she would attend the next Sui fair with him and her face reddened again. As she thought of him her heart started beating fast. When she called him at 10.20 p.m. the night before, she was told that he had gone to the palace for dinner. She felt jealous of his beautiful girlfriend, Kunwar Sita Devi, but felt helpless too.

She had fallen in love, without any care and did not know what would be the outcome.

She recalled her aunt's interest in the trip to Jote. Her aunt told her that in the morning, while playing cards, Sita Devi asked about Kina, but on her uncle's advice, did not reveal the fact that Kina had gone to Jote with Mian Sahib. They both wondered at Sita Devi's interest in Kina.

It was then that Kina discovered that Inder was the Chief Conservator of Himachal Pradesh and the son of Raja Davinder Singh of Bharatpur, a small royal state near Rampur. He studied at Mayo College in Ajmer and then went to other countries like New Zealand and England as a Foreign Service Officer. Her aunt told her that people wondered why, even though both royal families were keen on the match between Inder and Sita Devi, till date he had not decided to marry her, or his batch mate, Kumari Rama the granddaughter of the Raja of Sitarpur. The latter had visited Chamba with him a few times in the past and there was speculation about their early marriage. Rama Devi was more beautiful and a keen horse rider and tennis player like him.

'However,' said Kina's aunt, 'I found her too haughty and didn't like her. Then Sita Devi came into his life. But frankly, no one knows how many women there are in his life, because he is a rich, young royal and holds a position in the state.'

She listened to them, but didn't speak. She merely described his cottage; how expensively and tastefully it was furnished. Later, when her uncle left the room, her aunt asked her, 'What do you think of him?'

'I don't know,' she replied but couldn't meet her eyes.

'At times people do get attracted to people belonging to a different status with different personalities.' Kina recalled Inder telling her that her uncle was too good a judge not to notice the sudden change between them. She was glad he did not stay for dinner.

Her aunt continued, 'And my dear you're different. You have a charm that can attract any man.'

Bhola Ram was driving on a straight stretch of the road, with the Ravi flowing along the slope of the high, rugged, rocky mountain, without any trees or greenery. All along, the left side of the river was barren and rocky. She wondered why. They passed Village Mehla on the right. It was famous for the yatra (holy fair) to the temple of Goddess Hidhumba near the snow-fed river Rohru every year in October. During the three days of the yatra of Mahla, goats were sacrificed and meat was given as prashad. People came from long distances to attend this yatra, to enjoy the local fair, eat and drink the local wine and then pray. At night there were dances and folk songs around the bonfire in praise of the Goddess. The kind Mother was renowned for her blessings and the waters of the Rohru for its medicinal values. The famous song of Mahla was " 'Yatra Rohru the pani too Kala mat pinda, Dhol Sharabia.' (On the yatra at Mahla, the waters of the river Rohru must not be drunk by you," dhol in a drunken state.)

Ramu started singing and she was lost in the memories of her childhood and how she enjoyed the mela (fair). They were driving along the mountain on the right of the Ravi and after crossing the bridge arrived at Rakh, another small town on the mound, above the grassy green valley.

She fell sleep but woke up when the car slowed down on the side of a narrow road off the main highway, leading to a bridge over the Ravi and on to the temple of Trilochan Mahadevaji. She told Bhola Ram to stop the car and park it on the side near the tea stall. She got out of the car and walked down the narrow road with Ramu. After crossing the bridge, they entered the small hut-cum-temple with a single Shivalingum in the centre. The pujari was talking to some of devotees. She offered money to the deity, took the prashad and sat on a boulder looking down at the river, which almost touched the mound of the temple. But here again the mountain was rugged and barren. There was so much water but no forest, and it puzzled her. She thought of Inder, who being an expert would know the reason.

According to legend, this hut belonged to a boy, Trilochan, who took up tailoring as a profession, when his father died. He lived with his mother and they earned very little. One day, a handsome young Gaddi came to the hut and hired him to sew his Gaddi dress but only in his house. The boy agreed when the man promised to look after his mother while he was away.

The young Trilochan carried the Gaddi's sack of salt and followed him as he climbed up and down the mountains until they arrived at a lake. The man had an extraordinarily brisk style of walking and climbing and the poor boy had a hard time following him. The lake was at a height of 11,000 feet. He crossed the lake by walking on its surface. It surprised Trilochan, but when he tried, he too could walk on the surface of the water. Then the man started climbing up the highest mountain which was rugged and had a sandy surface with boulders and thorny bushes along the path. They finally reached the snowy peak, and the man told Trilochan to stay there and sew the chola (the traditional Gaddi dress).

The land in front of the snowy peak on the slope was grassy green and covered with fruit trees and flowers, in the middle of which was a beautiful hut. Trilochan entered and saw that it had everything he required. The man gave him the cloth and told Trilochan that he would return on the day the chola was ready.

'But how will I inform you? Trilochan asked.

'You cannot, but I shall come.'

The boy was worried about his mother so he worked day and night. The day he completed his task, the man entered the hut and tried on his chola. He was happy with it and praised him. Trillochan asked him to give him his money. The man laughed and said he had no money. He bent down, picked up the empty sack, filled it with leftover discarded cloth and told him to go. Trilochan was angry and turned to leave without the sack. But the man picked up some pieces of cloth lying on the floor and put them into the boy's pockets. This angered Trilochan, so he left the hut with the sack of cloth.

He took the same route he came by and arrived at the temple of Bhurmani Devi at Bharmaur. The small temple of Bhurmani Devi is still on the mound only a few kilometres from Chaurasi (eighty-four in Pahari), the sacred place in Bharmaur. There he decided to rest. A hunchbacked woman holding a walking stick emerged from the temple and asked him for some money. Since the boy was dejected he gave her the sack and walked home.

His mother looked happy and healthy. She told him that every day a man brought her some food and whatever she needed. Then she asked him about his payment and he put his hand in his pocket to bring out the cloth pieces but was surprised to see gold coins. He gave them to his mother and ran back to get his sack. However, he was told by the locals that the temple had been closed for several years.

When Trilochan did not return for six months, his mother decided to hold a feast. It is a custom in this land that if someone disappears for six month, he is declared dead and a celebratory funeral feast is held by his close relatives. However, he turned up on the day the feast was to be held, and described the route to the holy lake and the abode of Lord Shiva on the summit of Mount Kailash. But he disappeared again at night and they found his body at the confluence of the river Ravi and its main tributary, the Buddhal, at a place called Kharanmukh on the right bank of the river.

This is the place where one sees hundreds of pairs of new shoes of different sizes placed at one side of the bridge before crossing it. It is said that once eighty-four sidha yogis came to Bharmaur to attain moksha. Before crossing the bridge, they left their wooden slippers there, saying that this was the route to Lord Yama's land and those who donate their shoes there get to wear shoes when they cross the thorny passage to Yamaloka after death.

The people brought Trilochan's body to the hut, but when the white sheet was removed in front of his mother, they only saw a Shivalingum. This was established in the centre of the hut, which was made into a temple.

Lord Shiva then revealed that this man should be worshipped as Saint Trilochan Mahadeva and those who are not able to reach the holy lake, should bathe in the river next to the temple, after which they would receive the same reward from the Lord. A dip here was considered equal to one at the holy lake of Mani Mahesh. The local boys of the Sippi Caste (Trilochan was a Sippi), which is still considered a low caste, were, in accordance to Lord Shiva's order, made to lead the holy procession of the Mani Mahesh yatra from Bharmaur to Mount Kailash, and not the Brahmins, as is the usual custom. They were also the only ones who were allowed to swim to the centre of the lake, where the entrance to Lord Shiva's abode, Kalikund, lies.

Kina stayed there for a while, and then decided to resume her journey so as to arrive in time to attend the famous evening prayers at Bharmaur. Bhola Ram told her that he had seen Mian Sahib's motorcade going to Chhatrari.

'Are you sure?' She asked.

'Yes Madam, the white ambassador and the same jeep with guards was following it.'

She wondered whether he was imagining it, as he was not well. She told him to drive up to the Kharanmukh bridge, from where she would take over if he was still unwell. From Kharanmukh to Bharmaur is a short distance, but it is a very steep drive on a narrow road between a rocky mountain on one side and a deep gorge on the other. Since the driver had a headache and high fever, she took over the wheel. Driving up the hill on the narrow, steep road was scary.

Midway on the road, at a narrow turn, she saw a truck coming from Bharmaur being driven at a high speed. She slowed and blew the horn continuously, to indicate to the driver that he should stop at a wider part of the road, but he kept coming and stopped just short of her car. She lost her temper. She told Ramu to place some stones behind the wheels, parked in the middle of the road and came out. She started scolding him in Pahari and told him to reverse to a wider stretch. The man refused, saying that it was too dangerous for his heavy vehicle. She was now extremely angry and told him that she would see to it that he did as she told him, and stood in front of her car.

Though there was not a heavy rush, vehicles were piling up and drivers were blowing their horns. But she was adamant and refused to listen to the drivers who requested her to let the truck pass.

Then she heard a voice, 'What are you doing?'

'Just enjoying the weather,' she said without looking at the man.

'Kina, you're holding up the traffic at a dangerous site. Tell me what you are doing.' She turned and saw Inder.

'I shall not move if the driver of the truck doesn't do what I told him to.'

'Where is Bhola Ram?' She didn't reply! 'Now you're going too far and making me angry.'

'It is my decision. Why are you interfering? You are favouring that driver. Fancy driving so fast even when I repeatedly blew the horn to tell him wait at that wider stretch!'

'Now he can't reverse, because his vehicle is too heavy and there is the danger of it falling into the gorge.'

'I don't care.'

'Now compromise and allow him to pass. Just look at the number of vehicles increasing every minute.'

'No.'

'You foolish woman! You are stupid and brainless when you get into a temper. And now you are making me lose my cool, to the extent that I will have to be savage with you!'

'How dare you!'

'I shall show you. You fool, stopping at such a dangerous site on the main highway to cause an accident.' He pulled her off the car roughly and almost dragged her to the other side of the road. He made her stand next to a boulder and then said, 'Just move and I shall slap you this very moment in front of this gathering. I can't imagine how foolish and brainless you are to create so much commotion in the middle of the road.'

He saw Ramu and Bhola Ram standing near the car and said, 'Give me the keys.'

'Sir they are with Madam.'

He looked at her with blazing eyes and said, 'Give me the keys.'

She threw the keys to where he was standing on the road. His face turned red and his eyes were blazing as he took a step towards her, but stopped when the guard picked them up and gave them to him. He told Bhola Ram to remove the stones behind the wheels and to guide him. He parked the car on the edge of the hill, with just enough space to prevent it falling into the gorge. He then started regularizing the traffic first for those going downhill and then the ones going up. After the traffic was cleared, he looked at Bhola Ram's face and asked, 'Are you unwell?'

'Yes Sir, I have a high fever.' Inder called one of his guards and told them to sit in his vehicle and take Bhola Nath to the hospital at Bharmaur. He then instructed his driver, Bahadur, to drive his car and that he would follow. He drove her car up to Kina, who was now sitting on the boulder looking around. He told Ramu to sit in front in the passenger seat and ordered Kina to get in at the back.

'I shall drive,' Kina said.

'No you won't.'

'Then I shall stay here. It is my car and I will drive.'

He got out, caught her left wrist, dragged her to the car, opened the back door and almost pushed her inside. 'Just move and I shall spank you.'

He got in and started driving. 'You will repent this,' she said.

'I already do. Why did I meet you in Chamba? You're not only foolish, but brainless, more so when your fiery temper is ignited.

'You insulted me!'

'Not enough. I should have called the police and had you put behind bars for a few hours to teach you a lesson.'

'I hate you!'

'It does not worry me now because I am getting late for my meeting and am in a hurry.'

There was no more talk, and Inder concentrated on driving. The climb was very steep and rather dangerous for an inexperienced driver like Kina, he thought. However he was too angry to talk to her. Arriving at the top of the mountain, where there was an open space, called the khirkhi (window) on the right providing a vivid panorama of the beautiful grassy green valley on the flattened hill that had some houses, and beyond to the snow-capped peaks of the Dhauladhar Range. He parked the car next to his official car and called out to Bahadur, 'Take Madam to the civil rest house and after seeing that she is settled, come to the venue of the meeting at the forest rest house.'

He got into his own car and looked back. What he saw made him forget his meeting. Kina was standing in front of her car, her head covered with a scarf, eyes closed, praying. She looked totally relaxed. Then she bent down touched the sacred land with her hand and put its sacred dust on her forehead. She looked straight ahead at the highest peak, Mount Kailash, Lord Shiva's abode. She smiled and got into the car.

Inder returned to the present looked at his watch and drove off. A smile lingered on his face and he laughed as he looked back at her car following him.

The room Kina was given was next to the suite reserved for the Chief Commissioner. As she looked around the room, she saw one of Inder's guards bringing in a small bag, a suitcase and files into the suite. The guard re-arranged the furniture and after satisfying himself that all was well left the room. She was waiting for Ramu to return to tell her what time the prayer at Chaurasi was to be held.

Ramu had told her that the suite next door was furnished differently. It had a bedroom, sitting and dinning rooms and a very modern bathroom. There was a balcony on the other side with a view of Chaurasi. She thought that the senior officers certainly lived in luxury, but then looking at the travelling and meetings, she realized that they required the comfort to be relaxed and refreshed for the next meeting and journey in these remote areas.

She thought of Inder and recalled his blazing eyes. Now that she was relaxed she realized that she was wrong. But the thought that he wanted to hand her over to the police angered her. How dare he threaten her with the police! Her anger mounted further as she recalled how he had insulted her in front of his staff. She wondered why he didn't mention this official tour and then recalled his visit to the palace. The mere thought of it made her jealous and she decided to keep away from him. How foolish she was to think he had fallen in love with her when no sooner he left her, on the very same evening he met his girl. She was livid now.

She left the rest house at 7.30 p.m. with Ramu. Taking the narrow lanes up the slope between the school and other official buildings they arrived at Chaurasi. The sacred land and all the temples were being prepared for the evening prayer and the area was fully lit. Standing in the courtyard she looked at Mount Kailash but was disappointed that the peak was covered with clouds. Chaurasi was a cluster of ancient temples, surrounded by a wall with four gates. No one could drink alcohol, eat meat or perform any bad act here. In the olden days, even prisoners' handcuffs were removed when they passed through this sacred area. She went to the shrine of her Guruji. She climbed up the stairs entered, bent and made her offerings. She sat down, looked at the Guru and closed her eyes to pray.

As she emerged and was about to put on her shoes, she heard his voice. 'How is the fiery girl?'

He was standing close to the stairs, looking at her. She decided not to put on her shoes, which were near the staircase, and without replying turned to go to ancient temple of Mani-Mahesh, Lord Shiva!

'Still so angry Kina,' and laughed softly.

'Ignited!' she responded.

'Please don't poke your tongue out here like a monkey. Some of my officers may laugh at you.'

'Very funny!' and she entered the Shiv Temple. She bent down to pray when the thick voice said, 'Panditji perform a special puja for us.'

The pandit lit a diya and recited Sanskrit shlokas, so she was forced to stay put with him standing next to her, till the priest finished. He applied a tilak on his forehead first and then on hers and blessed them after offering the prashad. Kina left the temple and went into the courtyard. She saw that Inder was surrounded by some of his officers.

The clock struck eight and the temple bells started tolling. The entire courtyard was filled with people, young, old and not so old. Everyone looked at Mount Kailash and sang. The sky was clear but the highest peak was covered with clouds. She was disappointed that she could not see Shiva's abode from Chaurasi. The song resounded across the valley creating an aura of bliss all around the sacred city of Bharmaur. 'Shiv Kailsha ke Raja, dhauli Dhara ke Raja Sankat Sankat harna.' (The Lord of Mount Kailash, the Lord of the Dhauladhars bless us and take away our bad days.)

The arti continued with the bells tolling in each temple

and it created a most magical aura around Chaurasi. This name was given to the site when the eighty-four sidha yogis, lived there, prayed and sought salvation. It was actually not Chaurasi, because their leader, Charpat Nathji left soon after granting a boon to Raja Sahil Varman. The Raja had no children and was destined not to. When Charpat Nathji granted him the boon, he realized his mistake and left Chaurasi. The Raja had ten sons and one daughter, Champawati. However, with the death of Guru Maharaj Nanga Bawaji, the Chaurasi was said to be complete, because he was regarded as the reincarnation of Charpat Nathji.

It was getting cold and she was irritated with herself for forgetting to bring her jacket. She told Ramu that they would go home after visiting the other temples. As she was at the temple of Lord Ganesha someone at the back covered her with a woollen jacket and whispered, 'You are brainless aren't you? Fancy coming here without even a sweater!'

She was about to retaliate, when he warned her by raising his left hand. She stopped, and noted that he was amused.

'Now come, let us go back.'

'Not with you.'

'Well Kina, don't try me again.'

Just then a gentleman came up and said, 'Mianji I want to talk to you.' She got her chance to escape and told Ramu to return his jacket to the guard standing at some distance. They walked back the same way they had come. She was happy he was not there yet. It was freezing cold now, so she ordered hot tea and went to her room.

Chapter 5

THE ENTIRE Bharmaur valley was engulfed by the dark shadows of the high mountains, like sentries guarding the valley lit with electric lights. Kina looked at the lights scattered at different heights showing the presence of villages in such high remote areas. The sky was cloudy and it was bitterly cold. How unpredictable the weather in this part of the state was, she thought. The valley was at a height of over 7000 feet and was known to have snowstorms even in the summer months. As she looked around, she saw the snow-white peaks of the Dhauladhar range, even in the darkness. On a clear day she always thought of this place as a silver palace for the gods and goddesses. A sudden pressure on her shoulder made her turn. It was Inder.

'Why didn't you wait for me?'

'It was cold.'

'Is that why you left my jacket for me?'

'Yes.'

'Now let us eat our dinner.'

'I am not hungry.'

'Aren't you? How unusual for my Kina, even when she is so angry with me.'

'I am not angry!'

He didn't reply and went into his suite to order dinner for two to be brought to his dining room. She decided to go to her room, but he caught hold of her.

'Kina, now stop this drama, I know you're hungry. We will eat and then decide.'

He almost pulled her into his sitting room. It was comfortable and warm because of a fire burning in the grate.

'What do you want from me?' he asked.

'Nothing.'

'Look at me Kina, let's talk.'

'There is nothing to talk about.'

He laughed, 'So for the first time my girl has nothing to talk about.' He took her hand and said, 'You're still cold,' and placed a kiss on the palm. 'You rang up at 10.30 p.m. I was not there. My servant told you I had gone to the palace to dine. So Kina was not happy, slightly angry and jealous,' he said looking at her red face and laughing.

'Yes.'

'Look up or I shall do something that will make both of us the gossip of this rest house and then of this beautiful valley.'

Footsteps outside made her look at his amused face. She saw the glint in those eyes and got lost in them. The door opened and it brought them back to the present. He released her hand.

'Scared?' he asked and before she could say anything added, 'I hate you,' and laughed aloud. He stopped as the waiter put their dinner on the table and left. He made her get up and sit on a chair at the table. The aroma of the food made her hungry. Since he made no further move, she looked up and saw him looking at her with a meaningful smile.

'Something amusing you?'

'Yes! You're hungry my girl,' and laughed. She rolled a chapatti and was about to eat it but holding her hand he started eating it and asked her to make another. She suddenly forgot everything, relaxed and started eating. They then sat in front of the fire, sipping hot coffee, while the waiter cleared the table.

Inder rose from the chair, closed the curtains and came to sit next to her. He held her in his arms and said, 'Now shoot.'

'I am not interested.'

'Oh, that's not true. But all right, I shall tell you everything that happened last night, on one condition however.'

She looked at him and nodded.

'You will let me demonstrate as I talk without moving and will not interrupt,' he said as he came closer to her. Kina nodded again.

'After I dropped you home, I went to my rest house that is inside the palace. It is in the private wing of the palace. Since I am related to the royals it is reserved for me when I come to Chamba.'

'So convenient!'

'Don't interrupt or I will stop talking. When I entered the room I saw Sita sitting in front of the fire on the sofa. The room was warm and comfortable. She was wearing a bright red chiffon sari. You know how well-groomed she is, unlike you, you tomboy. Looking at her standing next to the fire, with her white, marble-like body so well exposed behind the thin veil of her low-cut choli, I was almost tempted to make love to her. Then I sat next to her on the sofa.'

Holding Kina very close he started kissing her. She tried to say something, but he interrupted her.

'Don't, I am just demonstrating to you. I kissed her forehead. She closed her eyes and I touched both of them with my lips.'

'But Ö'

'Stop interrupting. Then her ear-lobes and lips. Our passion rose and she was now in my arms. I started kissing her and her kisses started matching mine. You know how?' And he started kissing her again. 'The response was encouraging, like yours,' he smiled, 'and so her passion, as yours now is, equalled mine and I was lost in the magic. I forgot the time and everything around me except her.' And he caught both her hands firmly in his.

'Why are you holding my hands?' She was blushing furiously now, and feeling too shy to look up.

He smiled and said, 'I don't trust woman when they are ignited. Especially Kina—she can be unpredictable.'

'Then what happened?'

'As you interrupted me, so were we by a knock and a message that the Rajmata was waiting for me.'

'So?' she whispered her face red with passion.

'So I had to go but I was reluctant to leave. Sita told me that I must go and refused to come with me so, I left her and went to the royal wing. There I met the Rajmata who asked me when I planned to marry her granddaughter. I was fixed. I had to choose between the two because what had transpired a few seconds ago reminded me that she was not bad. Then I though of you!' He looked at her and both were lost in each other.

'I replied, that I could not marry her granddaughter. She asked me why and I said that I did not love her.

'But Ö'

'Stop woman; let me talk. The Rajmata asked me if I was in love with someone else, and when I replied in the affirmative, she asked me who it was. I told her that she was Thakur Shamsher Singhji's granddaughter and that her name was Kina. The Rajmata said, "Oh I know her, she is Bimla's daughter. She is not beautiful and used to be a bit of a wild and naughty tomboy." The Rajmata smiled and continued, "Yes, I have known for some time that this alliance, which has almost been forced on you, would not work. You are too naughty; a fun-loving bubbly personality and too smart and clever for Sita, who may be beautiful and good, but is rather dumb." She smiled and said, "So Sita was right when she commented on the way you were looking at Kina at the club. And then you were together at Sultanpur."

'I was surprised that she knew this, but the Rajmata just laughed. "Look Inder, love, murder and theft can never be kept secret. Let us eat dinner and then you will be free." And she hugged me.

'I knew then that I could not stay away from you. I ate

dinner, and realized that you would be going to Hudsar. I rang the rest house and discovered that you were booked in the forest rest house while my suite was booked at the civil one two days later. So I brought my programme forward, explaining to my officers that I had some urgent work in Shimla. I fixed my programme to match yours and arranged for our stay at this rest house. By that time it was past 11.30 p.m., so I decided not to disturb you.'

Looking at her with a smile he said, 'My Kina has been thoroughly loved and kissed. But didn't I convince you?' he laughed. 'How did you like my demonstration?' he looked at her and said, 'Tell me you love me.'

She looked at him with his head now in her lap and said, 'Yes.'

'Then why not say it Kina?'

She looked at him. His head was on her lap now and he was looking at her, waiting.

'Yes I love you Inder,' she said and hid her red face in her hands.

'So Kina is in love with me,' he said, removing her hands from her face and looking deep into her eyes. She nodded. He stood up and held her in his arms, and for some time there was silence.

Still holding her, he said, 'The department officers and staff are just waiting to hear the announcement of our union, because I always come alone. Once, I did come here with Sita, who accompanied me to Chhatrari to visit Goddess Durga's temple, but they could not see any close relationship between us. The royal visit was conservative, and perhaps I was not at all in love. It was nothing like the way I feel for you. And at times I find it so difficult to keep away from you, or to pretend. Just imagine Kina, even someone as dumb as Sita noticed the way I looked at you while she was playing cards. We must marry as early as possible.'

Then raising her face asked, 'Are you ready Kina?'

'Yes.'

He suddenly laughed, and she asked him, 'What is amusing you?'

'I just thought of the incident created by you in the middle of the road, when you were so angry with the poor driver. Don't you think this temper of yours could at times become dangerous, though it adds to your charm and I do love you so dearly,' and started kissing her again. 'I somehow don't want to have to speculate on what my wife might be doing in the future. But Kina will be difficult to control, knowing what she is like when furious.'

***

Kina opened her eyes when she heard the knock on the door. It was the waiter with the morning tea. She took the cup and wrapping herself in a Pashmina shawl went out to the veranda. It was sunny and she knew she had overslept. She looked at Inder's suite, which was closed and blushed when she thought of the night before. She turned towards the north-east and the snowy mountains. For the first time, Mount Kailash the abode of Lord Shiva was free of clouds. The clear darshan made her bend her head for his blessings. As she looked down she saw Inder in his khaki jodhpurs on his white stallion entering the compound of the rest house. She watched as he alighted, gave the whip to the groom and looked up as he turned towards the building. He smiled at her and waved.

He climbed up the steps to the veranda, kissed her cheek and took the cup from her hand, 'Let me have a sip of hot tea. Did you sleep well?'

'Yes.'

'Now let me tell you something.' He turned her around to look at the mountain. 'That road goes to the temple of Goddess Bani.' He pointed to the road running along the slope very close to the summit of the hill. 'It is motorable and so it is easy to visit the temple. I am taking you there. I have a meeting at the rest house at Bani village, and then there is a reception for me by the Gaddi and Gujjar communities of the area.'

'Oh!'

'They love me because I saved them from punishment for deforestation in Bani forest.'

'How did you do that?'

'I told them they could cut trees, but for every tree they cut they should plant two saplings. It worked. Then I got ill in the rest house with fever and cold. The Forest Department looked after me but the locals prayed for my early recovery and I grew close to Akbar Khan, the chief of the Gujjar community in this region. He is over ninety years old and predicted my early recovery, good health and also my future.' He smiled at Kina. 'That was the time when my buaji was after my parents to make an alliance with Sita Devi, and they were all waiting for my decision.

'Tell me about the prediction.'

'Hold on woman,' he said and kissed her lips. 'He said that I would not marry the royal but would fall for a simple girl, who was a commoner and that I would have a very pleasant and satisfied life with her. He also said that I would have one son.'

'We need to leave soon, so get ready for another adventure,' and he almost pushed her into her room.

They left at 10 a.m. with Inder driving the jeep and Kina sitting next to him. His official car with the driver and two guards followed. The road was not very wide, but it was cemented. The mountains beyond a certain height were covered with tall pine trees, but down below it was barren and rocky with only dry prickly foliage and boulders. Driving along the road, they had a beautiful view of the valley with the new housing colony and city of Bharmaur surrounded by high mountains. While admiring the view, Kina was lost in her thoughts of this man, so handsome, relaxed and charming and her being so much in love with him.

'So we are dreaming again,' Inder said with a smile.

It was cold even with the sun shining all along the mountain slope. They entered the valley, arrived at the snow-fed rivulet and crossed the small wooden bridge.

'This is all reserved forestland. No one can cut trees here, but they can build temporary shelters in the forest. At the top, below the mountain peaks there are green pastures, which are the delight of the Gujjars and Gaddi tribes. They graze their cattle and sheep there, which are guarded by their Gaddi dogs. You know Kina, the Gaddi dog is very clever and faithful to his master, and guards the flocks from wild animals ferociously. He is of the same size and has the same nature as the dingo of Australia.' Inder informed Kina.

They finally arrived at the small, single-storeyed rest house built from wood and river stones with a red tin roof and chimney. It was surrounded by green lawns, beyond which were the mountains. The view and serenity of the place were breathtaking. There was silence as Inder parked in front of the staircase and they entered the rest house.

Kina whispered, 'Tell me what you are thinking about.'

'Well I was looking at my love—how different from the women I met in the past. Yes I know you're my love now and forever.' He was about to hug her when she winked and signalled. A man came out and asked if they wanted tea.

'No,' said Inder, 'we will go to up to the temple before thinking about food.' He looked inquiringly at Kina, who nodded. He told the man and the guards, not to follow them as it was a short climb and he knew the area well.

'Sir what about food?' asked a guard.

'We will eat what the locals give us after the function, which is due to start at 11 a.m.' And turning to Kina said, 'So madam?'

She nodded and he lead her through the gate along the narrow track to the temple. The rest house was built by Raja Bhri Singh who was very fond of hunting. As they started climbing he held her hand and said, 'Tell me when you're tired and I shall carry you to the Goddess to ask for our union and blissful family life,' and bending kissed her lips. Holding hands, they started climbing, and Inder told her about the temple:

> The temple is centuries old, some say it was built in the fourth century AD, in view of the old architecture and woodwork, which till date has not been touched by termites. No one understands why this is so. It is just a wooden hut, with a small door. Inside, the deity is a block of dhatus (metals) some say seven dhatus. It is black but you will admire the one who crafted the mother goddess with beautiful eyes and sharp features, smiling at you.
>
> It is said that an old priest sat there and spoke to her in the presence of her devotees, most of whom were from the surrounding villages. He was sixty years old and his wife was fifty-eight, and they had no children. One day he got angry with the Goddess for the first time and said, 'Since you have not given us a child, who will serve you after our death?'
>
> That night he was awakened by the Goddess who told him to go to the forest surrounding the temple. He went. He was not scared as he had staunch faith in the Goddess.
>
> In the centre of the forest, he saw in the moonlight, a lioness feeding a human baby while another baby was playing with her two cubs. The children were twins. He stood behind the tree and watched. After some time the lioness left the babies and walked off with her cubs. He was asked to pick up the twins and return home. He did but was in a dilemma regarding the origin of the twins. The Goddess said, 'Bring them up as your own children and no one will even question their origin. Today, one of the twins is still alive. He is a hundred years old; the other died last year.

They arrived at the temple and entered. The old priest performed the puja for them and after applying the tilak and giving them prashad, blessed them. As they sat with him, he said, 'You will soon be husband and wife. You will have son and your life from now on will be full of happiness. The woman who tried to hurt you in the past can no longer do so.'

He looked at Kina and said, 'Do you believe in the reunion of souls?'

'Yes.'

'So you're united with the past and the two souls are happy now!'

He blessed her and they left the temple. They walked to the edge of the dense forest and sat on a boulder. Inder asked her if she believed the old priest and when she nodded he asked her why.

'Well you met many girls, all royals and beautiful and you couldn't decide, but with me you decided so suddenly. Why?'

He looked at her and nodded. 'Yes, you're right. I loved no one and they were so beautiful sophisticated and of blue blood. However, when I looked at you, the urge was so intense. That day at the temple in front of Bhairon at Chamba you asked me to pray. I lied to you, but I asked Goddess Kali to tell me what was happening to me. And then, although I had escorted Sita to the club, for the first time I performed an ungentlemanly act and left without her. This was on the mere urge to be with this girl, without caring what people would think. I got the answer when you turned and we were lost in each others eyes. Then something within told me to hold you, as you were my true love. I dared to hold you, kissed your forehead. I wanted you to stay with me but then at your request, I let you go. I sat in the car realizing for the first time that I had fallen in love. Though I tried to return to reality I couldn't face the other girl. I told her I was not feeling well. However at same time I wanted to see you again and saw you eating when our eyes met and I smiled. I couldn't rest, I talked to you Kina and then decided never to leave you.'

He took her in his arms and started kissing her. After a while, he looked at his watch and said they should leave. As they passed through the jungle he said, 'This forest is famous for two birds—the nilgar and phulgar. Their feathers are used by the royals on their official turbans.'

She touched his face and said, 'Do you have one?'

'Yes. You will see it when you go to the palace as my bride. I shall wear it for my Kina,' and laughed. 'No one ever hunts here before praying at the temple; otherwise you can never be successful in the hunt.'

The grounds of the rest house were full of people when they entered the gate. They were received by Akbar Khan, the elderly, tall Gujjar leader, while the air reverberated with the beating of drums and the playing of pipes and flutes, and the blowing of conch shells. Akbar Khan took Inder in his arms and looked at Kina. 'So she is yours.'

Inder nodded. Akbar Kahn stretched out his hand, held hers and said, 'I knew one day you would come here with him.'

The man took Inder to the central stage and made him sit next to him, while a young girl made Kina sit on a cushion placed on the hand-woven carpet next to the raised stage. She looked around and saw the men and women of the two nomadic tribes in their local dresses. The function started with a pink turban being placed on Inder's head followed by a marigold garland around his neck. A young Gaddi woman came up to the stage. She performed the arti and placed a tilak on his forehead. Then the function started.

There was a Gaddi dance and followed with a dance by the Gujjar girls. Periodic flashes of light from the rear made her turn and she smiled. The function was being televised. She saw someone go up to Inder, who looked at her and then nodded. There was an announcement that Kiran Kapoor would sing a song of the mountains. She looked at the man closely. She was surprised to recognize him as Sunder. He was in a Gaddi dress and she never expected to see him in such a remote place. She was not even aware that he was a Gaddi even though he sang with her on the local channel and radio so often. She only knew him as a handsome sophisticated man in Shimla. She rose and looked at Inder who smiled back with a nod.

Holding the mike and standing in front of the raised platform with Sunder and two girls, she nodded as one of the artists started playing the flute. She started singing and dancing in tune with the music, and for the time being, she was lost in the song.

Kangra di uchia ridia, Bansi bajanda ho, dhangra jo chara deranju minjo sade ho
Kangra di uchia
Chukia Gudoloo gori pania jo chali ho, Bansari dital usede dile lagi ho.
Kangra di uchia ridia Bansi bajanda ho, dhangra jo chara deranju minjo sade ho.
Rakhia gudoloo goria ghare jaike ama jo galandi aye kam kami ke.
Kangre di uchia. . . .
Sajna jo mili gori dhara jai ke, behai kari layee ja minjo ghare aye ke.
Kangre di uchia. . . .
Painia chaneba cchm 'chum ghare aiyo ho, leyee jana Ranjhu behai ghare aye ke.
Kangre di . . . Bansi di tal goria mane lagi ho
. . . Bansria d ital gori mane lagi ho.
Dhangra jo chara deranju minjo sadhe ho
Mithi mithi tal mere dile lagh ho.

(The young woman is lost when she hears the sound of the flute played by someone up on the high slope of Kangra. She tells her friend to look after her cattle. Picking up a pitcher and telling her mother she would fetch some water, leaves to meet the man. She returns with a promise that he will marry her and take her to his home as his bride.)

Kina refused to sing again but joined the Gaddi dance and found it amusing when they forced Inder to join them. The food was simple: maize bread, ludoo of maize steamed in a covered pot with butter, lassi (buttermilk) and a curry made of buttermilk and vegetables called kasrode, which is only cooked on the high mountains.

Following this, Inder told them that he would help them with their problems and took the papers to get things sorted out in Shimla. He accepted the present for his forthcoming marriage and with a laugh, as suggested, asked her to go inside and change into the clothes they had presented.

It was a green Gujjar dress with a silver necklace, ear studs and ornaments worn on the head. As she came out she felt very shy, but as suggested, Inder held her and kissed her forehead at which, everyone clapped and laughed.

It was past 5 p.m. when they left the rest house. 'So my Kina sings. What a melodious voice and those dancing feet!' He stopped the car, took her in his arms and said, 'How many other talents do you have to woo your man darling?'

It was past 9 p.m. when they reached the rest house. As they entered a man said, 'Sir there is call for you from the palace.'

He picked up the receiver and said, 'Yes, I did. Well I had to go to Shimla early and then of course I shall. Thank you.'

He turned to Kina and said, 'That was Sita Devi. She has invited me to dinner on my return to Chamba and then wants to go to Shimla with me. It seems either she was not told or is trying to pretend.'

Chapter 6

NESTLING AMIDST THE tall pines, oaks and deodars on the flattened top of the mountain in the north-west part of the city of Hudsar was the beautiful two-storeyed rest house of the Forest Department. The building was made of wood and sandstone with a red tin roof and chimney typical of the old British architecture. The British were clever in the way they built these places for the comfort of their officers to encourage more hard work and as an incentive to discover more natural wealth in the form of wood, minerals and wildlife.

Though the distance to this beautiful town of Hudsar was only fifteen kilometres, the road was a narrow, winding, steep climb with several small bridges over snowy rivulets. The high mountains all around were covered with dense forests, snow-fed rivulets and green foliage, so unlike some of the barren mountains of Bharmaur. These slopes were covered with foliage and wild hill flower of different types right down to the deep gorges, adding a wild beauty to the valley.

They lunched at the forest rest house at the top of the mountain, midway to Hudsar. Inder stayed back for a meeting with his officers, and told her to go on to Hudsar and rest. She observed that the officers were quiet and respectful, but, as Inder mentioned, they were waiting to find out more about her.

It was now evening and she looked at the north-west in anticipation of the first phase of the sunset, as an orange hue covered the entire town. She recalled her trip to Nepal where they had travelled sixty kilometres from Khatmandu, the capital city, to Hotel Everest to view the famous sunset and Mount Everest, the highest peak of the Himalayas. It was beautiful but watching the sun going down behind the snowy mountains casting a purple hue, this was just as beautiful. She wondered whether nature was different in different places and realized that it is the same everywhere. It was only the way of looking at it that made it different.

It was getting chilly, the lights were coming on in the small town and she could even see lights scattered along the mountain slopes. She thought of Inder. He was late. The temple bells started tolling in preparation for the evening prayer, after which they would be closed. A sound brought her to the present and she looked down to see his motorcade. Inder looked up and smiled. She waited. The sound of steps on the staircase made her turn, but it was his two personal servants with bags and files, which they placed in his suite. He must be busy with the people who were waiting for him when she arrived. A hand on her shoulder made her smile and she said, 'Inder you're late. Why?'

He didn't reply, kissed her left cheek and said, 'You missed me?'

'Yes.'

'Getting bold my Kina?' he laughed. 'It is cold here, let us go inside,' and taking her hand led her to the sitting room. It was warm due to the fire and he took her in his arms and started kissing her. The sound of steps on the wooden stairs forced him to release her and they sat on the sofa next to the fire. The waiter entered with tea.

***

They were sitting together after dinner and Kina felt that he was too quiet. She asked him if something was wrong and he replied, 'It is time to tell you about my past. These last few days were days of happiness and excitement with no time to think seriously about us except about settling down.

However you must know about my past, more so now that we are going to marry. You must listen to what I have to say and decide. I shall not blame you if you change your mind about me. But I shall never fall in love again or marry anyone, because I only love my Kina.' His hold tightened and he didn't allow her to move. Putting a finger on her lips told her not to talk and just to listen.

There is a small erstwhile hill state beyond Rampur Bushaher called Bharatpur. The capital town of this state is Maithli. I was born there as the second child when my elder brother was five years old. He was called Bharat Singh but in the state he was known as Yuvraj Singh, since he was the heir to the state. The state was rich in precious stones, apple orchards, dense forests with varied wildlife. My parents, unlike other royals, were conservative, so we were affluent even after the national government took over our state. We owned several houses and property, not only in Bharatpur, but also in and around Shimla. My father converted one of our palaces on the mountaintop into a hotel. It overlooks the snow-clad peaks of the mountains, where the three ranges of the Zanskar, Greater Himalayas and Dhauladhars meet at Kinnaur in the north-west. It is a delight for tourists especially the foreign ones, who come to India throughout the year. The hotel has a five-star ranking and was named after my brother Bharat.

My brother was sent to Mayo College in Ajmer to study where I joined later. I was very naughty, but simple and innocent, and very protected by my parents and then in school by my brother, who unlike me was conservative and quiet, but proud of his royal heritage. I was good in studies and loved horse riding, tennis, swimming and was fond of reading and debating. Yuvraj loved riding and in time got me interested in polo. We were always close and enjoyed our holidays at Bharatpur. He also taught me football, but I was not interested.

When he graduated from high school he went home and then decided to settle down and not to study further. He got engaged to Asha Devi the niece of the Raja of Kinnaur. Since I was good in studies I continued and decided to become a bureaucrat. I joined St. Stephen College in Delhi. Twice a year we attended polo matches at Jaipur. Our favourite place to stay was the Oberoi hotel. Here one day I met a girl, Rheena Kumar. She was very fond of horse riding. She was beautiful, tall, fair, with a willowy body and a broad face. She had Rajasthani features and a glowing complexion. She knew how to lure young men like me and I fell for her. Yes she was my first love and I was so mad about her that I even thought of giving up my studies to get married and live with her in Bharatpur.

My close friend, Rajender Kumar, came from Jaipur and told me that she belongs to a zamindar's family in Jaswantpur. They were paupers now and Rheena was known to be a social flirt and blackmailer in college. We had a major fight and I stopped talking to him. I started spending more time in Jaipur and more money on her shopping, parties and hotel stays, and periodically gave her money to repay her father's debts. He was an alcoholic and had sold most of his land. Rajender Kumar was a good friend so I think he informed my brother. He came to see me one day, apologized, and we were friends again.

On one of my trips to Jaipur, he called me and told me to meet him at the Trident hotel. Since I was meeting Rheena in the afternoon, I agreed. He took me to restaurant and selected a corner table to have a coffee and talk. We were talking when I saw my brother walk in with Rheena. He had his arm around her waist and even kissed her, which was so unusual for him. Rajinder turned and said, 'Oh he is her new man; appears to be very rich, and is a frequent visitor. I believe he is the son of a rich royal family from one of the small hill states. He has bought a beautiful new fiat for her.'

'Do you know the man?' I asked.

'No,' he said and I heaved a sigh of relief that he didn't know the man was my elder brother. I went to the hotel, where Rheena and I were to meet. She told me that since her father was not well, she had to drive down to Jaswantpur. She asked me for money. I gave it to her and despite her insisting that I should not, I accompanied her to the gate. When she showed me her red Fiat, I asked, 'Who gave it to you?'

'My cousin Thakur Balwant Singh of Dharampur,' she replied. I nodded without telling her that I knew that family well. Thakur Sahib was over sixty years and a strong family man.

I returned to college and decided to work hard to become something in my life and started studying. However Rajinder warned me to be careful as she was very good in blackmailing and had already done considerable damage to two rich boys' families in Jaipur. He advised me to pretend to be busy, give her money till I qualified but on no account should I meet her alone if she invited me.

I qualified for the Indian Foreign Service and went to Mussoorie, happy to be posted out there. One night she rang from the Savoy hotel in Mussoorie. She had come to see me. I made the mistake of agreeing to dine with her and then paid the bill as usual, gave her money for the hotel bill, but refused to be alone with her in her room and left. I was sure by now she was convinced that I was no longer interested in her, and I was in any case due to leave for New Zealand within a week as Third Secretary in the Indian High Commission. Rajinder met me that night. He was posted in Jaipur as a junior IAS officer in the Home Ministry. He was worried and asked me why I went to meet her alone. I told him I was scared of her coming to the academy.

In the morning I received a phone call that a girl called Rheena Kumar had lodged an FIR against me for raping her. Rajinder and I went to the police station. She was alarmed to see Rajinder but kept crying and blaming me. I was nervous, but Rajinder Kumar insisted on a medical test. This was not done till he said that he would approach his uncle IG Promod Kumar of Dehradun. The test was negative but she threatened to put a report it in the newspapers and see to it that my posting was cancelled. Rajinder took his uncle's help who informed my parents. The very next day my brother came. He didn't meet me but suddenly all was quiet.

I tried to meet my brother who was now with Rheena in Delhi but he refused and I discovered that the day before my departure he married Rheena. My parents came to Delhi and were sad that I was leaving. They did not mention my brother and Rheena but insisted that my nanny go with me to Auckland to look after me.

I was a shattered young man, but Auckland is a most beautiful place, and my work and interest in sports kept me busy. I started hating the female sex, and was called the most unsuitable bachelor of the embassy. I had a good time and enjoyed my skiing holidays, received regular letters from my parents but they never mentioned my brother.

Time passed and I was posted to England and was promoted to Second Secretary. I liked the countryside, Scotland and Ireland. Once, on a holiday I fell ill and was admitted to a hospital in Belfast. There I met a young nurse, Nancy Smith, and I got interested in her. By now I was sick of my lonely life so decided to marry her. However it ended when my mother rang to tell me that Yuvraj was not well and there was a suspicion that he was being slowly poisoned. I left London and got a posting in Delhi. We had a family get together without that girl, my bhabhi, who was now living in a house in the city given by my father, but enjoying frequent trips to Jaipur while her son was left behind, with the nanny or her parents. My brother was pale, thin and very sick. We were worried and then he was diagnosed as being slowly poisoned with cyanide and rat poison. I looked after him and he regained his health.

When the family decided to go to Bharatpur, he decided to stay a little longer in Delhi with me. He left for Bharatpur after a month, when I was informed that he had disappeared between Kumar Hati and Solan. We were alarmed and I contacted Rajinder Kumar. He was now Commissioner at Bikaner. Together we decided to teach this girl a lesson, thinking she might have kidnapped him.

I think my brother's disappearance made her happy, and for the first time she took her son with her to meet my parents who had not accepted him as their grandson. Though he was named Bhupinder Singh, he also had his father name as Yuvraj's son.

One day Rajinder rang and told me that my file at Misssoorie was reopened. His uncle told him to get it closed as soon as possible because he had discovered that an Inspector Bhupinder Singh was now a close friend of this girl and he had reopened the file which was now in his custody. However, when the Inspector heard about Rajinder's uncle, he panicked and told her to leave things till all was quiet and not to open the file again. She was told that the case was too weak and if it was not proved she could go to jail for defaming a senior IFS officer.

Rajinder's uncle also suggested a DNA test for the paternity of the child and collected personal information about the girl, the date of her rape, as she claimed and the date of the birth of the child. At the end all was proved. The child was not premature, he was a normal full-term delivery at the local hospital at Jaswantpur so she was pregnant four months after the date she had accused me of rape. The gynaecologist at Jaipur where she went to terminate her pregnancy was known to Rajinder and she extracted Rheena's papers and the name of a man Ravinder Kumar, the only son of a rich jeweller who was her boyfriend came to meet us. He said that he didn't want Rheena to terminate the pregnancy and wanted to marry her but she refused. The DNA test tallied with Ravinder Kumar's who was honest and ready to give evidence and the case is now in the High Court at Shimla.

Rajinder started searching for Yuvraj. It was interesting to learn that he had discovered that my parents did not appear unduly concerned about the disappearance of their son, and while he suspected Rheena, Yuvraj was not at Jaswantpur. Her father confessed that his daughter had a bad character, but drew the line at kidnapping.

Now darling, there is this woman, my brother, whose whereabouts are still unknown and her son is, whatever you may say, a part of our family. Over and above, I am known as a man who has had many girlfriends and is now guarded by security men wherever I go, to save me from Rheena. But I am in love with you and want to marry you. So what is your decision?

He looked at her and said, 'What a mess.'

Kina laughed, rose and looked deep into his eyes and said, 'Shall I tell you?'

'Tell me Kina.'

'Do you really want to know?'

'Damn you woman tell me.'

'Oh, so my darling is impatient!'

'Yes! Talk or I will spank you!'

'Well I shall marry you now, tomorrow, or any time you decide and without any care,' Kina said and kissed him. 'Don't worry I am sure Rheena will repent one day. That is the saying of Saint Kina.' She flung herself in his arms and he started stroking her head softly. She did not know when she went to sleep, but when she opened her eyes she was on the sofa covered with a blanket and he was nowhere to be seen. She smiled and went back to sleep because it was not yet dawn.

Chapter 7

THE SOUND of a horn made Kina run down the stairs to the car. She was late. Sitting next to him she whispered, 'I am sorry.'

There was no response. She looked at him and felt shy as he was looking at her.

'What is wrong?'

'Nothing.'

'Tell me.'

'Your outfit suits you.' She was wearing a green loose kurta of pashmina wool over matching tight pyjamas and was carrying a matching shawl.

'Well Kina sleeps without knowing where she is and talks.'

'I don't.'

'You did last night as you went to sleep in my arms and I also dozed off. My arm under your head became numb and I awakened. I realized you were cold, so I covered you with a blanket and went to my room.'

'What about my talking?'

'You murmured that you loved me.'

The road to the temple was narrow and steep. When they arrived she found a rocky area with boulders all over, in the middle of which was the small temple. It did not have an ordinary temple structure; it was just a small square room painted yellow. There was a single wooden door and it was dark inside, even though an oil lamp was burning. The room was filled with the aroma of burning incense and because there was no window it was filled with smoke. In the centre was a metal image of the two-armed Lord Shiva. So unusual instead of the Shivalingum. It had a human face with sharp features, beautiful eyes and it smiled as it looked at the devotees. The one arm held a rosary and other a fruit. She wondered at the fruit, it looked like a mango or guava. The deity was sitting on a high pedestal made of stone which had an inscription: 'In the year of bliss, 14th of Jyeth, here Bhagasyoni Nathu's sons Gangu and Kisanu built the Mahadeva at Harsar'.

She whispered, 'Tell me what is the true name Hudsar or Harsar?'

He looked at her, her head covered with a muslin scarf almost covering half her face said,' I call it Hudsar, and you look like my bride.'

The priest was the old man Inder had mentioned. He was in his indigenous long, woollen kurta and tight pyjama instead of the usual saffron dhoti. He wore a Pahari cap and a muffler was wrapped around his neck. He took the packet offered by Kina, opened it and then placed the golden canopy in front of the Lord. He recited Sanskrit shlokas, put a saffron tilak on her forehead and offered her prashad. It was then Inder's turn to receive the blessings of the Lord. She noticed that he was also wearing the local dress but over that he wore his suede jacket for warmth. She smiled as they came out of the temple.

'Is something amusing you?' he whispered.

'Your dress but it suits you.'

'Am I not the most handsome man? Everyone tells me that. Women look at me with lusty eyes and tell me they love me, but not Kina.'

She nodded. 'Yes! You are a handsome man; you are also a ladies' man,' and laughed. He came close to her and holding her hand said, 'We have to climb that steep stony road. It goes to Danccho. It is a very steep climb, rocky and full of thorny foliage. However we have to walk only half a kilometre to see Sanchi Maharaj.'

She nodded and they started out. On the way he said,

'Danccho is a beautiful place, more so after the tough climb. At times one has to crawl like a monkey,' and pinched her nose. 'The small hill town has sparse inhabitation, mainly Gaddi. It is at a height of about 8000 feet and so is very cold and under snow for nine months. There is another temple of Lord Shiva there with a big Shivalingum, which is close to a frozen waterfall. There are natural falls of snow called Kasheer falls. It is said that Lord Krishna's abode lies below the falls. So devotees bathe under the snowy cold water prior to their journey to Mani Mahesh. The legend is that after Janamashtami Lord Shiva left his abode at Kailash and went to the lower world called Patal and from that day the land was looked after by the Lord of the Universe, Lord Krishna. Why are you looking at me as though I am telling you something very rare?' 'I always saw you as a modern man and I am admiring you because I realize that you are also religious, practical person with a humane heart.'

'So Kina has started admiring me!' Their eyes met and they were lost for a while. The cold wind brought them back. It was now getting cloudy and Inder said, 'Kina walk fast we must meet Sanchi Maharaj.'

As they climbed up the left side of the rocky mountain they saw a white flag. The track was extremely narrow, with both sides covered in thorny foliage. It was a kuchha road and full of pebbles, which made it difficult to walk. Suddenly it widened and became smooth. Just up ahead they saw a big cave, cut into a large boulder.

'This is where Sanchi Maharaj lives,' Inder said. 'And on top is the small temple with a Shivalingum. As they came up to the boulder, she saw a tall man emerge from the cave. He was over six feet tall and wearing a saffron dhoti. He was light complexioned and had blunt features but large blue eyes.

He smiled at Inder and said, 'I knew you were coming and I was just waiting for you.'

Kina noticed that he had beautiful white teeth and looked

less than fifty with a wrinkle-free face and large reddened eyes. There was peculiar shine on his face and his thin athletic body made him look young. He bent down and invited them into the cave in Pahari. It was spacious and airy. An oil lamp was burning in front of the deity, whom she recognized as Lord Buddha. It was made of a yellow metal and there was a gold canopy over his head. Incense was being burnt, but unlike at the temple, there was no smoke. Kina looked around and discovered a small hole in the roof, through which natural light entered. The floor was covered with a carpet and there was a fireplace in the centre, where a fire was burning.

He sat facing the deity and signalled them to sit on the carpet across the fireplace. He spoke in a slow, soft voice in Pahari.

'So you have come to wed here?' She looked at Inder, his face reddened and he nodded. 'Wait for a month,' the holy man said. Looking at her with those big red eyes and faint smile on his face, he continued, 'She was your wife in the last janam (birth) also. Do you believe in rebirth or reincarnation?'

She nodded.

'The wedding can wait for two month. I told you the last time we met, that when I talk, you will listen and that will be our last meeting.' He smiled at Inder. 'The woman who is troubling you at this moment is trying hard to get your inheritance. She is beautiful, young and knows the value of physical attraction. You know her better by now. You have undergone enough trouble at a young age. It was your destiny and no one could have helped you. But she is evil. These days her stars are against her. She is surrounded by servants who are from the secret service watching all her movements but she is unaware of this. I must say your mother is very clever. These days your nephew is with her. What a nice boy, but he is not well at present. Your older brother is alive. He has recovered from the poisoning and has married his beloved and is waiting for a suitable time to show himself. He is with your mother's brother but you must not talk about him till the time is right. The woman who tried to attack you but failed, is still planning, hoping to get half the inheritance. She is trying to declare the boy as yours, but all the evidence will be against her, though she is not aware of this. She will soon file a case, but she will not only fail to prove anything, her son's illness will break her. But in the end, all will be well. There will be an attack on your life.' He then smiled at Kina, 'So you are a surgeon. Get engaged only. This is not the right time for your wedding though a friend is waiting in the temple.'

Kina looked at Inder, he nodded and she asked, 'Can you tell us the reason why we should delay the wedding?'

The Maharaj brought out an old hand-made cloth bag and took out a black thread with a green stone. He told her to come closer to him and he tied the thread around her neck.

'This will save you! Now listen carefully. She will come in disguise to your hospital in the month of November to make a final attempt to kill you, so that Inder, who loves you, will be devastated. The day will be dark and it will be snowing. She will wear a dark green sari, and it will be the first time you will be meeting her. You will have no clue who she is. She will tell you she had a fall and hurt her left palm, which will be covered with a white dressing. She will smile and request you to see her in your office. Don't get up. Just press the bell while talking to her nicely and when your nurse comes tell her to open the dressing. You must then leave with an excuse that you need to wash your hands. Don't listen to her but leave the room as soon as possible because in her bag she will be carrying a poisonous snake which she had brought to bite you. She will ask for you and the nurse will press the bell for you, but don't return. Leave the hospital and ask the guards to get her bag, but not to open it till all is safe.'

He turned to Inder and said, 'She will not touch you now, because her plan is to get her son declared as yours and then be part of you. All will be well at the end. The future for both of you is smooth and happy. You will marry in the land of your birth have a son in August next year, and he will be the owner of half the inheritance of Bharatpur, because your brother's boy will be there and your brother will be happy again.'

Then he turned and looking at her said, 'You wish to know how old I am? I am 160 years but I will be no more today. This will be our last meeting.' He laughed. 'I was asked by the Almighty to help Inder so I waited. He is good man and will prosper. I bless you both. Yes you are in love. And so the two souls of the past have met in this janam,' and laughed.

He took out a fruit and to their surprise, they saw that it was a guava. They wondered how it could grow at such a height. He cut it into two, gave one half to each and told them to eat. As they did, she saw a sudden change in the man—he looked very old now with a wrinkled face and no teeth.

They heard a frail voice, Goodbye Inder. Leave the cave and don't turn back to look inside. I am going now. I was only waiting for you.'

They rose and left the cave. The return journey was quiet and she wondered at the magical sayings of the saint. They reached the entrance she saw that there was no white flag. She pointed it out to Inder, who only nodded, because his eyes were misty. The guards were waiting down below and they followed them to the temple. On the way Inder wondered who was the girl her brother had secretly married and then smiled. 'It must be Asha Devi the niece of the Raja of Kinnaur. They were together before his marriage to Rheena and I always thought they were in love.'

She looked up at the sky it was clear but the winds from the north-west were icy. Looking at the temple and seeing a red Fiat she said, 'Inder there are some people there like us to make offerings to Lord Shiva.'

He held her hand. 'Kina, will you wait? Will you marry me after two months?'

'Of course.'

'If I say marry me now?'

'Now? But Sanchi Maharaj told us to wait.'

'Yes. So you also believed him. We will wait two months. The wedding will be held at Bharatpur and he smiled at her. Then his hold tightened and he whispered, 'Rajinder is inside waiting for me to witness our wedding!'

'Oh, why didn't you tell me?'

He laughed and said, 'Even during the last few minutes I was doubtful. But then I always knew within me and trusted my Kina. There will be no one else from now. Never mind the delay, life ahead is ours. "Inder with Kina, what a surprise!" That is what the royal world will say. So what shall we do? We will get engaged today and marry as he said after two months, though I am disappointed that tonight will not be our wedding night. At times I wonder how I shall live without you.'

They entered the temple, a man in casual clothes sitting in front of the deity rose and turned to Inder who hugged him and turning, said, 'Kiran Raj. Her name is Kiran but for me she is Kina. Come Kina and meet my friend Rajinder and you already know all about him.'

Rajinder was plump with a round face and blunt features. He was not very tall but there was something in his personality; he had honesty and the quality of a friend to depend on.

He smiled and looking at her said, 'This time I agree with him that his girl has everything he wanted in life. He told me this on the phone the day he met you in Chamba before leaving for Bharmour. I must call you my bhabhi soon after this short ceremony.'

He looked at Inder and said, 'Your wedding in front of

Lord Shiva is to be kept a secret for some time?'

'There will be no wedding for two months as Sanchi Maharaj has instructed us.'

'I am glad. And I shall tell you later, but first let us finish our work here.'

He went to the corner of the temple and called out to Pandit Hari Ramji. 'He is our family priest in Jaipur.'

A man in a white dhoti and silk kurta covered with a shawl came in with the same temple priest. The temple door was closed and a fresh fire was lit in the small grate in front of the deity. The incense sticks and oil lamp were placed in front of the deity with a box of sweets and fruits.

'Panditji it is not a wedding but an engagement ceremony.'

Pandit Hari Ram sat next to Rajinder while the old priest took out his book and asked the couple to stand in front of the fire. He asked Inder to hold her hand and chanted some shlokas. Rajinder then rose, took out a ring and gave it to Inder. It had a large diamond with rubies and emeralds studded around it. He asked for her left hand and then slipped it on her ring finger.

'This ring now belongs to my future wife. It was kept in the treasury at Bharatpur and meant for the wife of the chhotÈ Yuvraj to be taken out by the Rajmata, my mother, at the time of my wedding,' Inder said, and his voice was hoarse. 'My mother gave it to me when I was going to New Zealand but I left it with Rajinder.'

Kina realized that he missed his parents. 'She will be there when we wed.'

He nodded, 'I hope so!'

'You should believe in what the saint, Sanchi Maharaj said, Inder.'

'Well I shall do so Madam,' and he laughed.

Next, a band was given to her and she put it on his left ring finger. Then the panditji from Jaipur chanted some shlokas, after which he put saffron tilaks on their foreheads. He asked Inder to touch the top of her head, which he did and he blessed them. After touching the deity the two stood for some time with closed eyes while the panditji continued the shlokas. The entire ceremony lasted half an hour.

'So today you're engaged,' Rajinder said looking at Inder, 'and I approve of this alliance.' They left the temple at 4 p. m. and Rajinder whispered that the priest was paid enough to keep his mouth shut.

As they came to the town, Kina asked Inder, 'Can I buy something? I shall only take a few minutes.'

Inder asked the driver to park the car on the side. Kina went to the shops and in hurry bought local hand-made socks, mufflers and gloves, two silver bracelets, two pairs of red and green earrings, one gold pendant with a chain. As she turned to leave the shop she caught sight of hand-made caps. She bought two for men and one for herself.

***

At tea Rajinder told them that though he came, he was worried that their wedding may be discovered by the people in Shimla. 'I knew that your brother was poisoned and his brain was affected. That is why your mother with the help of her brother made him disappear at Parwanoo. They took him to a private hospital at Mumbai. He was sick and confused, so he stayed in Mumbai where they treated him and suggested that he be kept in a safe place under nursing care. This was done at Rampur and then at Kinnaur. Now he is fully recovered and just three days ago, your uncle took him to Shimla. He is staying in your house in Chhota Shimla. The Bharatpur house is under the protection of guards and Rheena is not allowed to enter or come anywhere near you. That is why I am glad you have postponed your wedding.'

'Does this woman know?'

'No it is a top secret, which is why your mother is not at Shimla. My suggestion is that you go to Shimla and help him get a divorce.'

Rajinder then took out a medical report and a letter from a shop in Shimla where the powder was purchased. 'The shop sells indigenous medicine, but she bribed him and got the poison. It is located in the lower bazaar of Shimla and is very small. The police has the evidence.'

'How did you do that?' Inder asked.

'Remember Ram Chandra Sharma at the Academy? Well he is now Deputy Inspector General of Police in Shimla. I met him in Jaipur and he promised to help. All this information is from him. And he is still there to help you. Anyway I am happy that you have got me a beautiful Bhabhi.'

They decided to leave the next morning and for Inder to go to Shimla the very next day, to help his brother.

Kina brought out a small plastic bag and gave it to Rajinder, saying, 'Whenever I visit a new town or city it is my habit to buy the indigenous products of that place. So I bought a few things for you. Though they do not amount to much, it is just for you to remember your visit.'

He opened the bag and found a pair of socks, a muffler, a cap and a plastic box. He opened it and saw two beautiful silver kangans and a note. He read the note. It said: 'Though we had not met before, this is a small token for the woman who should be proud of her husband with so many qualities and a man I admire for being so dependable for his friend in adversity, Kina.'

There was silence, Rajinder replaced everything in the bag, rose and told Inder, 'Don't be jealous but I must kiss the future bride and my Bhabhi,' and kissed her left cheek. As she looked up she saw he was touched and his eyes were misty but then he laughed, looked at his friend and said, 'Thakur Sahib is jealous.'

She turned to look at Inder and was lost as he was looking at her with a peculiar expression. To create a distraction she turned to Rajinder and said, 'I think you're right, The royals are unpredictable,' laughed and left the room.

Inder followed her. She put the gold chain with the

pendant around his neck and said, 'The lord Shiva will protect you as the local jeweller told me. Inder don't ever take it off.'

He nodded and holding her said,' I love you and that will be forever.'

Chapter 8

SHE ARRIVED AT HER uncle's house at 6 p.m. She warned both Bhola Ram and Ramu not to talk about the journey to Hudsar knowing her aunt could get all the information she wanted from the servants. She was surprised to see her uncle and aunt sitting in front of the fire in the sitting room, instead of getting ready to go to the club. Both were very involved in club life. They looked pleased to see her and told her to relax and have a hot cup of tea. She sat near her uncle and said, 'Somehow I can't believe that the two clubs birds are sitting at home. There must he something very important, or is someone coming?'

Her uncle said, 'These women are unlike you Kina. They are a different species. They are keen club goers, card players, gossipmongers, fond of eating food outside and of quarrelling, but it is all done with style,' and he laughed.

'It seems something has happened during my absence.'

'Yes. And it was a hot topic here,' her uncle said.

'Really? Tell me,' Kina said, looking at her aunt.

'Did you meet Mianji on this trip?' her aunt asked.

'Who is Mianji?'

Her uncle said, 'She is talking about Thakur Inder Singh!'

'Oh, I thought it was Mian Sahib, the officer at the civil rest house!'

'I booked a room at the forest rest house for you,' her uncle said.

'Yes, but there was some meeting, so they gave me a room in the other rest house. There was a sudden change in

Thakur Sahib's programme and the officers were in a dilemma. Yes! I met Thakur Sahib,' Kina said and started laughing. She told them about the episode of the traffic jam between the bridge at Kharanmukh and Sanjoli. How she held up the truck driver for almost half an hour to teach him a lesson, when Thakur Sahib took over and sorted out the mess. She narrated the story with great spice and made them laugh.

'He must be amused,' her uncle said.

'Amused? He was too angry to talk. Do you know what he said about me? He said, "Fancy a female driver on the road and how I detest them. They make a real nuisance of themselves and create trouble." '

'I have never seen him losing his temper,' Uncle said.

'Then try him with me,' and she winked.

'So what happened?'

'He made poor Bhola Ram, who was not well, drive, and like a police inspector warned me: "Madam, one more such act and I shall see that you are held by the police for days." What a mighty man!'

This time her uncle laughed. 'Did you apologize?'

'No and why should I? There was a conference in the forest rest house and he helped us get place in the civil rest house.'

'The guard was right, then when he told me that all Sahib's official tours were pre-poned suddenly late at night. So instead of going with me to Sultanpur he left at 4 a.m. on the same day you left Kina. It must be very cold now.'

'Yes, but the place was comfortable at night. Now any further questions?'

Just them Ram Dyal entered, looked at Kina and said, 'Madam a police inspector, Harish Gupta is here to see you.'

She looked at her uncle and said, 'I hope he has not booked me,' and winked. But her uncle thought it could be something serious so told her to stay put and went out. He returned with a plastic bag and said that Mianji had left this packet for her on his way to Shimla!'

Kina opened the plastic bag and seeing both their eyes on her, she turned red. She looked inside and said, 'Oh this is the shopping I did before the arti at Bharmaur. Since it was late he gave Ramu and me a lift to the rest house. I forgot this bag and left for Hudsar early the next morning.'

'So you didn't meet him again Kina?' her aunt asked.

'We must believe you Kina,' her uncle said and winked at her.

'Very funny,' said Kina.

'It was even funnier here,' her uncle replied. 'Let your aunt tell you why she is so upset.'

Yesterday afternoon there was a small function at the club and we decided to play bridge. I was surprised when Sita Devi joined us and asked about you! I found it slightly unusual but replied that you had gone to Hudsar to make the offering given by your mother at the Shiva temple. 'Very religious girl,' Sita said. I couldn't understand her remark and replied that you were not religious, but your mother was, and being the only daughter you always abided with what your mother wanted.

'I believe she is a doctor,' Sita said.

'Yes,' I replied, 'she is a specialist surgeon, just retuned after three years in Australia and England.'

'These days girls are very adventurous. They look around and try to grab the best man as their husbands to enjoy a convenient and comfortable lifestyle,' she remarked.

I decided to keep quiet and wondered at her talking like that to me. Then she turned to Mrs. Kamal Chandra, and said, 'There are some girls from ordinary families these days who are more interested in our royal setup. They don't know our royal traditions, customs or style of living, which is so different and intricate that only royals can survive in such circumstances. Well our men are very unpredictable about their loves and choices about whom to settle down with. Though they enjoy their fling whenever available.'

Mrs. Chandra asked her about Mianji and she said she had called him at Bharmaur. 'He is on an official tour and will attend the dinner tomorrow that is to be hosted by the Rajmata. After that we will go to Shimla,' and gave me a meaningful smile. To tell you the truth, her loose talk appeared slightly childish. That was why I was a little upset. Because I felt she was specifically talking about you Kiran.

'That seems rather strange. Poor me how can I, a stranger, suddenly become part of your gossip? Now I remember Sita was looking at Mianji frequently that day at the club and then he left suddenly and returned after a long time. Then again he left the girl he brought with him. Don't worry aunty everything will be fine.'

'It appears very simple to you. This is a small town and rumours spread fast. The poor Rajmata, the guest of honour for today's dinner, left Chamba.'

'The police inspector told me that Mianji had left Chamba too and on the way he brought this bag. Her uncle looked at Kina and continued, 'Did you know Kina?'

'No.'

Her uncle and aunt were both looking at her inquiringly. She looked straight back at them, took a last sip of tea, rose, and saying that she wanted to bathe, left the room. She remembered Inder telling her about the phone call from Sita Devi in Bharmaur. She looked inside the plastic bag and thanked God she had not opened it in front of her uncle and aunt. There was a beautiful, expensive, brown pashmina shawl, a pair of silver bangles and an envelope. She opened the envelope and found a photograph of the two of them outside Lord Shiva's temple, and he was holding her left hand. She remembered this was taken by Rajinder

Kumar and at that time she felt too shy to stand with him. At the back was a note: 'As I send you this photograph I must say I love my bhabhi, but the man standing next to me is missing her badly, Rajinder.' There was a folded piece of paper, and it said: 'Darling I love you be there at 10 p.m. you will receive my call. Hope you like the bangles. Do wear them when you get them and you will know I love you. Inder.'

So the royal is in love with an ordinary girl and she smiled. She joined the couple for dinner after her bath and to give them prashad from the temple of Shiva at Hudsar.

'Kina show me those bangles.' Looking at them her aunt said, 'They are beautiful. I never knew you even cared to wear such jewellery.'

Looking at her husband she said, 'I think your Kina is changing.'

Kina recalled Inder saying that her uncle was a very good judge and would know if there was a sudden change of attitude between them. At dinner, her aunt told Kina that her father called in the morning and told them that he and her mother had moved to a bungalow in Sector 18 in Chandigarh for six months as the doctors advised that she must not live in the hills.

'Oh, that means I will go to Dalhousie only to close the house and then on to Chandigarh. Not bad. Now I can join the hospital at Shimla earlier.'

'I am sure you will be happy there. Shimla is beautiful and so good for young people in love,' her aunt smiled. Kina decided to ignore her remark but turned her face away. It was red and she went to the bay windows. She decided to go out and gaze at the lighted valley, to avoid further personal questions.

She stood next to the railing. The valley was dark, but the sporadic lights from the huts produced a beautiful sight. She heard a flute being played and she was lost in the tune of 'Chanchlo'. She understood why the people of the hills wanted to live and die here. There is love with solitude, a serene atmosphere, and every corner arouses your romantic emotions. It was cold and no one was around. She thought of Inder, touched the kangans and looked at her watch. It was not even 8 p.m. Thinking about her trip with him made her smile.

She wondered how her uncle and aunt would react if they discovered this romance. Well, she thought, it would finally be open knowledge in two months or even earlier. She was glad that she took off her ring as Inder had insisted she wear it only in his presence. She thought of Sita Devi and smiled. Inder was staring at her all the time that day, so she must have noticed. The royals still consider themselves different from others. A soft cough brought her to present. It was her uncle.

'So you are dreaming Kina?'

'What do you mean?'

'Well you were deep in thought when I came. May I ask you a personal question?

'Yes, of course.'

'Are you interested in someone you want to marry?'

'Why do you ask?'

'You know I love you and since your childhood you have been my favourite niece, so I am curious.'

'Well, I don't know, but the moment I am aware of it I shall tell you,' and Kina touched his hand.

'Somehow I have an intuition that Mian Sahib is interested in you! Your aunt is simple but Kina I am a good judge and suspect that something is going on between the two of you. Those bangles are not available at Bharmaur and are not of ordinary silver. They reveal an expensive royal touch.'

'Oh. Uncle, can we end this topic?'

'Well if you say so, but on the day it comes true, I shall be very happy. I liked Mian Sahib. He is a royal but unlike the others. He is down to earth in his manners and hospitality.' The sound of a flute started her humming the song,

'Chanchlo'. He joined her, and they started singing together.

The phone ringing interrupted them. A servant came up and told her that she had a call from Chandigarh. Kina looked at her watch. It was not yet 10 p.m. She picked up the receiver. Her father was at the other end. He told her to close the house and come to Chandigarh, but not to worry, as all was well there.

Kina got into bed waited for his call. When the telephone rang, it was Sita Devi.

'Kiran,' said the voice at the other end. 'You don't know me but I wish to warn you not to try to come between me and Thakur Sahib. If you do, you will get to know me very well.' And the call was disconnected.

Kina was extremely upset. The phone rang again. It was Inder.

'How is my Kina darling?'

'Well.'

'You are very quiet Kina. Is someone in the room?'

'Yes.'

'We have just arrived and not even entered the bedroom of this beautiful Circuit House! I miss you but did what you asked me, not to travel at night. This is second order I have received. How many more are to come I wonder.' He laughed and continued, 'Well I can't talk any longer, Rajinder is waiting. Love you.'

***

It was past 6.30 in the morning in Chandigarh. Kina had spent two week with her parents and finally, when they asked her to leave, she decided to do so. She threw off the quilt and dressed in jeans, a thick pullover and a woollen cap. Sitting in the rear seat of the car, she reminded Bhola Ram to drive carefully, and then sat back and relaxed. She took her final view of the 'City Beautiful', with its well-maintained, wide roads, well-kept parks and incredible cleanliness. The city nestling amidst low hills with its unusual architecture designed by le Courbuisier, was divided into sectors and had a beautiful university, lake and the Post Graduate Institute of Medical Research (PCIMER), one of the finest medical institutes in the country. That was where she had initially wanted to do her post-graduation in surgery, but changed her mind and soon after a house surgeon's job in Delhi left for Adelaide, to do her post-graduation in plastic surgery.

She was lost in thought when Bhola Ram said, 'Madam Sahib called from Shimla, this morning and told me to come to the road leading to the Tara Hall School by 12.30 p.m. I didn't tell you earlier, because senior Sahib and Madam were with you!'

'Good.' She smiled at the thought of seeing him again after three weeks. It was so difficult to dissuade him from visiting Chandigarh and alarming her parents. He was getting too possessive, but after another few weeks they would be together.

The warmth and sun made her lazy and she went to sleep. The car slowing down awakened her. She looked around and saw that they were on the bypass to Solan. She told Bhola Ram to stop the car near the next tea stall. After tea, she told him to drive straight to the road to Tara Hall.

'Do you know where it is?'

'No Madam but Sahib told me his guards would be there.'

'When did he take your number Bhola Ram?'

'At the cantonment in Chamba from where he left for Shimla. He took the numbers of Dalhousie and Chandigarh.'

She decided to keep quiet. The drive was beautiful and it was a straight stretch till Khandaghat, from where the climb up the Shimla hills started. She looked at the grassy valley below and the mountains scattered with pines trees between which were rocky and barren hills. At a farther distance were the snowy mountains. The sky was covered with dark clouds and it was getting cold. She wrapped the small car rug around her. She regretted leaving her woollen jacket at Chandigarh, but smiled when Bhola Ram said, 'Madam Senior Sahib put your jacket in the car.'

She smiled again on recalling her father's words: 'Somehow my Kina has changed after her visit to Shiva's temple. It seems Lord Shiva has blessed you as he blessed us when we got you after eight years of marriage.'

'What do you mean?'

'I have an intuition that you won't be with us for long, and won't be wild and free as in the past. I think you will settle down with a handsome man soon.'

'Why do you say that?'

'I am reminded of what an astrologer in Chamba once said. He said that my daughter would not marry any ordinary man. She would marry a rich royal who would love her equally.' And he smiled and gave her a meaningful look. She wondered if her uncle had said anything, but decided to change the subject and started talking about them buying a house in Chandigarh so that they could spend six months of the year there. He then told her that he was excited about one particular house and was negotiating the price.

It was past 1 p.m. when Bhola Ram slowed the car and said, 'Madam, Sahib is waiting.'

The car stopped and he walked up to her, opened the door and said, 'You are late Kina.' 'Yes.'

'All went well?' She nodded.

'I was getting worried. Who knows what sort of commotion Kina might have created on the way,' he said, and holding her hand helped her out of the car.

'How wonderful to see you after three weeks,' he whispered.

'Where are your guards?'

He laughed and pointed to them.

'Where are we going?'

'Oh woman can't you wait?'

He turned to Bhola Ram and said, 'Go home tell Nanny we will be there at 6 p.m.'

'Yes Sir,' Bhola Ram said with a grin.

Inder escorted her to the front passenger seat, took the

driver's seat and said, 'To celebrate our meeting after an interval of three whole weeks,' and started driving up the slope.

'I missed you, even though my brother, mother and Asha Devi are here.'

Glancing to the rear, he stopped the car. Putting his arms around her, he kissed her forehead and said, 'I did miss you darling.' He released her and continued driving.

As they approached the school he took a left turn and descended the hill. It was a narrow, kutcha road and he drove carefully. He turned to the right, drove for a short distance and stopped in front of a green wooden gate, which two guards standing there opened. He drove on to the next gate which had already been opened and stopped the car in front of a beautiful, small, wood and brick cottage with a red tin roof and chimney. The cottage was on a flattened hilltop, surrounded by lawns, which were not very green but appeared well cared for. Two men in grey uniforms and green turbans were waiting there. One of them opened the door for him.

'How are you Ram Singh?' Inder asked the man.

'Your Highness,' said the man as he saluted him.

Inder greeted the other man in the same way and walked over to open the door for Kina. 'Welcome to our cottage Kina.'

Holding her hand he looked at the two men and said, 'She will soon be your Chote Sahib's wife.'

The two men come forward and bent down in front of her. Kina was terribly embarrassed, and as she glanced at him she saw him looking at her with a peculiar glint in his eyes. Then holding her hand he led her to the front lawn and the edge of the hill.

'Close your eyes Kina and then turn and read what is written on the front.'

She opened her eyes when he told her to do so and read: 'Inder Kina Cottage.'

She couldn't believe it and without a care put her arms around him and kissed his cheek. 'They are looking at you,' he whispered. She turned but there was no one in sight.

He laughed, 'You're getting rather bold darling.'

Holding her around the waist he showed her the view of Shimla.

'I bought the cottage two weeks ago and was just longing to bring you here. We will visit this cottage frequently,' and he started kissing her. After a while he looked at his watch and asked, 'Hungry?'

'Yes!'

They walked into the cottage and he whispered. 'Both these men have been my personal servants since I was in school. Ram Singh's wife Kanta will look after you personally. Though she is not very young, she is healthy and experienced, and will be good for our future ones.'

'Oh you!' she blushed.

'Well we will be married soon and will have a family so why feel shy?' And looking at her red face laughed. 'You know I am waiting for that night.'

The cottage was beautiful, expensively furnished and in exceedingly good taste. They ate lunch and then holding her he took her to the covered glass sitting room. She liked the blue wall-to-wall carpeting and the heavy red velvet and lace curtains covering the bay window, the beautiful heavy oak sofa sets with red and blue seats. She laughed at a photograph on the wall of her standing with Inder in front of the Shiva temple. The room was warm because of the fire in the grate.

Sitting close to her he said, 'I shall tell you something but first listen and don't laugh or I will stop and you will regret it.'

Resting her head against his chest, she listened as he started talking while stroking her hair.

That morning I had to go to Chamba for an official tour. I decided I must end this Don Juan style of life and settle down as a family man. So I started thinking about the girls around me. They were all from royal families well known to our family. I opted for Sita Devi as she is less talkative and more compliant. She is beautiful but not as clever as Roma Devi. Sita, I thought, was mischievous enough, yet docile and dumb enough.

Every royal, even educated ones like us, think about how the new bride would adjust to our royal customs and traditions, and be able to live within the norms of the zinana, if required. I rang Rajinder; it was late at night and he was not amused. However we talked and he told me not to be in a hurry but listen to my heart. The next morning I packed the shawl and two kangans with my clothes and left Shimla.

I had to dine at the palace first, so I left my bag in the car. Sita looked so beautiful and sexy in a red sari, and I was so attracted by those black eyes, that I decided to make love to her and propose marriage. But while we were sipping our coffee, and just as I decided to come closer, I recalled Rajinder's words, not to be in a hurry. So my plans flopped.

The day your driver damaged my car I was returning from Jote. I knew that the royal family was visiting the Sultanpur retreat so decided to go there. I saw her again, as she was there for the weekend with her grandmother, and had coffee with her.

Then I saw her in Jodhpurs. She had been out riding and had just entered the house. The outfit didn't suit her plump body and I noticed that without make-up, she did not look as attractive, so something made me wait. Driving back, I stopped to sit on a boulder and look at the paddy fields, wondering why I was being so indecisive. A sudden noise made me look down. I saw a girl in faded jeans and a loose red pullover! So rude, so angry and slightly unusual! Though I was very amused I can't say that I was attracted to her! I decided to irritate her further, so sat inside the police cabin to watch her reaction. And it did excite me.

I went to village Udaipur to worship goddess Durga and prayed to her to help me decide my future.

On my return, I saw you again at the Circuit House, and observed you closely. I decided to avoid you, but you even started haunting me in my office and I couldn't concentrate on my work. Then to avoid you I rang Sita and went to the club with her. As I took my drink I saw the same person in a different attire, sitting on a chair, not caring that she looked so bored. 'She is so different from this sophisticated world,' I thought. I was mesmerised as I looked at you and could not even hear what people around me were saying. I laughed when I saw you beating your ring on the glass and still recall your uncle saying, 'Poor Kina. She is a wild animal caged by her aunt.'

Your aunt turned to you and said something, and you nodded, placed the glass under her chair and made such gestures that your aunt signalled a warning to you. You nodded again, and then the face you made when Sita Devi ignored you, was far too amusing for me. I saw how you called the waiter, took a glass of juice held his elbow, and gave him a tip which he put into his pocket. He then smiled and took you out through the side door. You looked for your uncle at the door, but saw me make a face at you. You were annoyed and poked your tongue out. I knew then that I had to be with you. The urge was so strong that I disregarded all manners towards that sophisticated society just to be with you, and the rest you know.

I asked the Goddess to help me decide because my feelings were not under my control. So she did, when I placed a kiss on your forehead. That action made me realize that I had fallen in love with this wild monkey with a fiery temper, and scatterbrained to boot.

Then holding her in his arms, he started kissing her. They were lusting for each other, when the clock struck 5 p.m. Inder rose and suggested a cup of coffee. He rang the bell and coming closer to Kina, asked, 'And how did you like my story?'

'It was beautiful,' she replied and kissed him.

'Now let me tell you about the problem at Shimla,' Inder continued. 'My official house where I live is currently full of family members – my brother, uncle and now my mother and future bhabhi, Asha Devi. Several royal members, who are still engrossed in the court case are also there.'

'You are kept very busy,' Kina observed.

'Well, yes and no. Won't you ask me where I live?'

'No,' Kina responded touching his face gently, 'not till you are free.'

Inder suddenly became serious. 'Sanchi Maharaj told us that my brother was married. It is true Kina, though my family has not told me. I saw her coming from his room this morning when I was going out for a ride.'

'That is good. But what about the other woman?'

'Now she knows everything except what evidences we have collected. She knows about her husband and I believe she tried to contact him, but he is not allowed to pick up the phone. Then she tried my office and failed. She came to see me at home with her son, but the guards refused to let her enter and then the police issued a warning.'

'Did you see the boy?'

'No. After she received the notice for the divorce, she wrote to my mother saying that if my brother did not withdraw the case she would make the child's life miserable.'

Holding her, he laughed and kissing her, said, 'I am not na . . . ve, but an ungentlemanly, conceited bureaucrat.'

'We must go Inder.'

'Why?'

'You know why.'

'Ah yes, my mother,' Inder said as he got up.

Kina rose, and touched the back of his neck. 'You're wearing that necklace,' she said.

He smiled, 'Yes, I am wearing the necklace Sanchi Maharaj gave me. You know, when you gave Rajinder all those things I was jealous. Oh Kina, when can we get married?'

'You decide.'

'I shall. Just let this mess get cleared. But we can be unconventional like my brother and marry in front of this fire.'

'How are things with you in the family?'

'I am close to my brother now. He is quiet and protective towards me. My mother, on the other hand is very clever and I am slightly scared of her and her inquisitive eyes. She has already asked me about this band, but I was saved by a phone call. I have no doubt that she will ask again, and I will just say that all is well.'

'Inder tell me where did you buy those beautiful bangles? When I received your bag with the shawl and bangles and you wrote that I must wear them for you, I did. My aunt and uncle were surprised to see me wearing bangles, and my aunt admired them. But after dinner, as I was enjoying the view of the valley, my uncle came up to me and said that he had a hunch that I was in love. It was dark on the veranda, so I could just tell him to leave the matter, but he persisted. He said "These bangles are not ordinary ones from Bharmaur." '

'Oh my Kina was in trouble,' Inder said. 'I told you that he is an extremely experienced and wise man.'

'Those bangles were given to my nanny in Jaipur, when I was one year old. We were on our way to Pushkar, near Ajmer for my mundun. We have a house near that sacred lake – Bharatpur House. The shawl was given to me by my mother when I left for New Zealand. She received it from my grandmother when I was born. When my nanny died, she gave the bangles to my mother to gift it to my bride; not to her own daughter Bindu, whom I regarded as my close relative, and is now married to our cook. He was the one who discovered the source of poison given to my brother.'

They left the cottage together. He accompanied her to her cottage and told her to call him at 10 p.m.

Chapter 9

KINA WAS AT A loss one Saturday morning as she did not have to go to work. The sky was clear and it was a sunny day though the cold winds made it slightly chilly. She decided to visit the Tibetan market near Snowdown Hospital. There were several local shops selling goods from different parts of the region around Shimla, but her favourites were the Tibetan women sitting on the pavement. She bought a shawl for nanny, a woollen jacket for young Ramu and hand-made woollen socks for both of them.

As she turned towards the ridge she saw a blue Benz standing on one side of the road and Inder escorting a young girl clad in a blue silk sari and a matching pashmina shawl. He opened the rear door for the girl and once she was settled in, he sat next to the driver.

Three days had elapsed since their last meeting in the cottage. Whenever she called him, she was told that he was in the office. On the one occasion that he picked up the phone, he said that he was busy with his family and cut the conversation short. She assumed that there were people around.

Suddenly Kina felt excessively lonely and depressed, so she cut short her shopping spree and told Bhola Ram to drive home. She ate her lunch and went to sleep, but Nanny awakened her, saying Inder had come to meet her. She went up to the summit of the hill above the cottage. He immediately took her in his arms and said, 'Kina, you saw me today?'

'Yes, and if you saw me why didn't you look at me?'

'My mother was there and these days she is extremely inquisitive about this gold band. However soon everything will be sorted out and you will meet her. I am now sure that my brother and Asha Devi are married! It appears as though I am surrounded by relatives and problems connected with the court cases. I hardly have time to ring you, leave alone meet you, and I miss you.'

'So you were too busy with these palace women?'

A slap on her cheek made her look at him with sudden surprise. His fair face glowed red with rage and his eyes were blazing. For a moment there was silence. Then he pushed her aside and said, 'One more word from you again I will push you down the slope. You a common woman! You talk to me as though my family comprises concubines and I am a product of that! How dare you!'

He rose and started walking off, when Kina said, 'Please Inder, I don't doubt you.'

'How dare you take my name,' he retorted and slapped her again as she held his elbow to hold him to her.

'Don't ever dare to touch me damn you,' he said furiously, and pushed her so hard, she fell down. He climbed down the slope without looking back, entered the cottage when Nanny opened the door, and slammed it shut.

For some time she sat there not knowing what had happened. Nanny came up to her and lifted her off the ground. She looked at the blood on her salwar and said it needed to be cleaned. Kina walked down the slope but was in a daze. What made him lose his temper?

Nanny asked her what had happened in the evening.

'Nothing,' Kina replied.

This incident shook her faith in Inder and she wondered if what had occurred in the past was a dream. She called him on his personal number. The phone was picked up, but disconnected. When she called again, no one answered it. She decided to call at night. He had told her as he laughed and kissed her, that this number would unite them wherever he may be.

Her phone rang in the evening. But it was not Inder. It was Lucy from Christchurch, New Zealand. It was a pleasant surprise and Kina was happy to hear that she was married. 'I married your favourite anaesthetist, Dr. Michael. I followed him to London and then New Zealand and we are together now, married and in love. I rang you to tell you that his brother Tom Rice is in India. I have told him about you. He is in Agra and will come to Shimla the day after tomorrow. He is taking a ride on that romantic train, the 'Himalayan Queen'. He will be staying at the Cecil hotel and I have given him your number. He is a renowned urologist in our hospital so you can arrange for him to give a lecture there.'

Kina was happy for Lucy. It appeared that if you persist, you can get anything. She recalled Lucy telling her about Michael – young, quiet and dreamy. Kina tried to invite him for a coffee or dinner to bring the two together, but he usually declined, and even if he did come, he rarely spoke to Lucy.

Thinking about them, she decided to call Inder. He picked up the phone, but no sooner did she say, Inder Ö' he interrupted her in a cold voice and said, 'Don't waste your time and mine. I am no longer interested in you,' and banged the phone down. She redialled, but a servant picked up the phone and told her he had left for dinner. She looked at her watch; it was past 10 p.m. Her conversation with Lucy made her try his office. She was told that he was in a meeting and not to disturb him in future.

She decided then, to keep her distance from him. Dr. Leena told her about women in the palace: 'Palace women were concubines for the royals, but they can be compared to prostitutes.' This was the first time she understood the meaning of the word 'concubine'. She wrote a letter to him and sent it through Ramu. He returned and said, 'Sahilb tore the envelope without reading its contents and told me not to come to his office unless I had a personal problem.'

'So this is the end,' Kina thought. 'Look Kina our cottage "Inder Kina cottage." What a joke.' She took off his ring and placed in its box to return it whenever he asked her and got busy preparing a programme for Dr. Rice's three day visit to Shimla, especially to please Lucy. She made him an official guest to the medical school to give a talk on his favourite topic in urology, to spend time with senior medical students and staff. She also arranged a sight-seeing trip of Shimla and a dinner at the Cecil with the senior medical staff of the hospital. For some time, she forgot her depression and took more interest in her practice. She gave a talk on the local channel on the importance of early repair of congenital defects which were common in Shimla. The talk pleased the medical director.

It was past 2 p.m. when a thick husky voice on the phone introduced himself as Dr. Rice and asked when they could meet.

'When did you arrive and where are you just now?' Kina asked.

'I arrived this morning by train and enjoyed the journey thoroughly. I have checked into the Cecil Hotel,' Tom Rice replied.

'I will meet you at 4 p.m. this evening and show you some parts of Shimla.'

'Great, I look forward to meeting you.

She wore her black woollen slacks and thick red sweater, and kept a long coat, woollen cap and muffler in the car. She entered the hotel lobby and as she arrived at the counter, a man came up to her and said, 'Kiran?'

It was Tom Rice. They shook hands and he said with a smile, 'Call me Tom. Lucy described you so well I had no problem identifying you.'

They laughed and she said, 'Let's go. I'll show you Shimla by night.'

'At your mercy ma'am,' he responded. 'Lucy calls you Kris. May I do the same?'

'Yes.'

They got into the car and she told Bhola Ram to drive off. She turned to Tom and laughed, 'You're too tall for this car.'

'Oh, the train was worse from Kalka to Shimla, but the view was breathtaking. And this place, with its snow-clad mountains, dense forests, the sound of flutes and these beautiful people is just too much.'

She laughed and said, 'Wait till you see the hill maidens,'

'Yes, I have seen one,' he said and smiled at her. She suddenly felt embarrassed but ignoring the remark asked him if he would like to climb a hill.

'The best view of this city is from Jakhu hill at on attitude of 2,445 metres. In ancient times our God, Hanuman (the Monkey God) is said to have rested here on his way from the Himalayas.

'Let us go,' he said, 'if you don't mind climbing!'

She laughed, 'I am one of the best trekkers of these mountains. I come from the hills of the north-west.'

She turned to look at him and was again embarrassed to notice that he was watching her. She asked Bhola Ram to stop near a shop and wait there. Together they started climbing. 'You were telling me about the Monkey God.'

'Oh, yes! He was on his way to Lanka with a small herb, and rested here for a while. The plant called Sanjiveni, was needed to save Lord Rama's brother, Lakshman, who was injured in the war between Ravan the Raja of Lanka and Lord Rama. Ravan had kidnapped Rama's wife Sita. There is temple of Lord Hanuman on the summit and you will see many monkeys there guarding the temple.'

When they reached the summit, she continued, 'The city was initially a small hill village (Shimla) discovered by an English lieutenant, Boss, in 1819. It became the summer capital of the Raj from 1864 to 1947 and now it is the capital of the small hill state called Himachal Pradesh. There is an airport, but you came by train from Kalka a small town in the foothills, about 167 miles from Shimla. Now look down at the city. It stretches out for about 12 kilometres, down the mountain.'

She pointed out to a spot and continued, 'That spot is called the Ridge. That is Christ Church built in 1844 by Colonel J. T. Boileau. This is where Rudyard Kipling whose father was the Principal of Mayo College in Lahore started writing about Shimla during the Raj. That is the Mall, the main shopping centre with many restaurants. Looking westwards along the Mall you pass the Roman Catholic Cathedral. I think it was established in 1885. To the north is Annandale where they held several picnic and fetes during the summer, but now it is under the control of the army.'

She pointed out the mountain ranges in the north-east.

'Fascinating; and the guide is excellent, besides being beautiful,' Tom said.

'Thank you,' she said.

While he took photographs, Kina observed him. Lucy was right. He was, tall and good looking with an athletic physique, unlike most New Zealanders who were plump. He had a lean face and deep blue eyes. She wondered why he was not married.

When he was ready to leave, they walked to the Ridge and down on to the Mall. At the point where the Ridge meets the Mall, in front of Lala Lajpat Rai's statue, she stopped and said, 'This is called Scandal Point.'

'Why? Something wrong with this man's character.'

'No. he was one of our freedom fighters from Punjab. The handsome, dashing Maharaja of Patiala abducted the beautiful daughter of an English gentleman and took her to his palace at Chail, a hill station about 42 kilometres from Shimla. Nothing happened because the lady didn't complain, and all was fine with them but the spot was named Scandal Point.'

Tom took a photograph and laughed, 'What happens if I kidnap you at this point? I think it will become a second scandal point,' and they both laughed.

They walked down the Mall and then to the lower bazaar. 'Come I will show you Shimla at night and we will have our dinner there.'

'Alright at your service madam,' and he held her elbow as they entered the restaurant Davico. It was early, and the band was playing soft Western music. They sat near a bay window at a table for two from where they got an all-round view of Shimla and the well-lit gorge. They ordered apple juice and the waiter opened the windows. Kina described the layout of the city beyond and he took some more photographs. He then turned to Kina and asked, 'May I have one of you Kris?'

She smiled her agreement and he took a picture of Kina pointing to the highest light on the top of the mountain.

'Thank you. It has been wonderful meeting you!'

She started to smile, but froze as at another bay window her eyes met those of the man she had been trying to talk to for over a week and a half. He was sitting with Sita Devi and holding his drink while she studied the menu. Their eyes met but she saw no warmth or expression on his face and he turned away. Kina decided not to think about it then, and smiled when Tom took another photograph of her. She then requested the waiter to take one of them eating together. Then he got up and said, 'Kris now wave. This one is for Lucy.'

She laughed but then stopped as a side glance showed that Inder and the woman were looking at her.

'Why bother with them,' she thought and started telling Tom about her drive with Lucy to Murray Bridge with no water in the radiator of their Morris 10 car, and how the policeman thought they were not only deaf but also dumb.

'Why?"

'Well it was our first long-distance drive. Lucy had just got her license and bought this old car. It was hot on our return journey and the car was smoking. We heard the sounds of a helicopter and police siren, but since we were talking, we ignored them. We were stopped by a policeman ultimately. He asked Lucy to open the bonnet but she could not. The policeman told us to get out of the car and asked us why we were risking our lives by driving the car without any water in the radiator. We were so shocked we could not speak and then he asked us if we were deaf, dumb or both,' Kina concluded and they laughed. They left the restaurant and Kina noticed that Inder had also left. The waiter gave her an envelope. She wanted to tear it in the same way he had torn hers, but opened it and read:

Today I have finally assessed you. You now have a new name 'Kris'. You're worse than the palace women. How many others are waiting in the background for you to play with?

Inder.

'Something wrong? You are looking very agitated,' Tom said. 'I can assess Kris,' he said, holding her hand. 'I have found a new friend in you. Look up, those tears show that someone has hurt you.'

'Yes,' she said, then laughed and said, 'Let us see some more of Shimla, before I take you outside the city.'

'That's my girl! Let me tell you something. Keep your head held high in all seasons, but more so when there are dark clouds. The storm may blow, but you must never lower yourself or run away. Stand and fight like I did,' Tom said with a laugh.

But Kina suddenly saw sadness in those blue eyes, and she nodded, touched his hand and said, 'Kris will always be Tom's close friend.'

***

The next day they drove to Naldehra, 23 kilometres from Shimla.

'Your lecture was good.'

'Thank you, but I doubt you understood anything, being a plastic surgeon.'

Kina said, 'I love surgery but get bored and irritated watching the best plastic surgeons carrying out repairs as though they are walking on crutches.' She made a face and laughed.

'Laugh more often Kris, it suits you.' He then inquired, 'Tell me about the Indian dress you are wearing.'

'It is a dress worn by the Gujjars, a tribe that live high in the mountains. They wear these clothes with heavy silver and multicoloured bead jewellery. They are nomads, and travel between the dense forests and high peaks, making their temporary shelters on the pastureland, where they graze their cattle. I will now show you a place in Naldehra where there is a nine-hole golf course on the top of a flattened hill at a height of over 7,500 feet. It is surrounded by cedar trees and is very beautiful.'

She pointed down the deep gorge with the river Sutlej flowing through it, and the famous sulphur springs called Totla Pani.

'Naldehra has a temple of the Snake God Nal. It is funny that Lord Kitchener named his daughter Alexandra Naldehra. You can see cedars, oaks and pines everywhere in this region, but there are only cedar trees surrounding a temple of the Snake God.'

She made him take a picture of a Gujjar girl, they ate lunch and decided to visit Wildflower Hall.

'It used to be Lord Kitchener's official residence and is now converted into a hotel and tourist spot. It is situated at a height of over 7,500 feet and is just the place to revisit the grandeur of the bygone British era.'

Tom took several photographs, and they were enjoying themselves, when suddenly as he was taking her photograph, he saw a black snake near her. He quickly pushed her and she fell and grazed her left wrist. She paled when she saw the snake, then rose and smiled, 'The God of Death doesn't want to take me yet.'

She was touched when she observed that the man was so concerned about her that he placed a kiss on her forehead and said, 'Oh my God I could have been the cause of your death,' and became so emotional he could say no more.

They drove to Kufri, where they drank tea. Though it was winter Kufri was free of snow. Kina took him shopping. He bought pullan (shoes) made of grass, two saris, a thick Tibetan pullover and a Kulu cap. She bought a Pashmina shawl for Lucy and a pati (woollen coat) in a brown and beige check for him.

Kina returned to the cottage around 7 p.m. and she dressed in a sari after months. She wore the black silk with a pink and white Jaipur print given by her mother on her birthday.

As she looked at herself she knew the sari suited her – but then Inder had never seen her in this outfit. His name reminded her of his note and it brought tears to her eyes. He thought she was low, perhaps because she gave her love too soon. He even compared her to his royal concubines and that made her furious. She arrived late at the Cecil Hotel. The small dinning hall was booked for the hospital staff and as she entered, everyone was waiting for her in the lobby. Tom Rice was in a black suit and white shirt. He was certainly a handsome man.

Tom looked at Kina and recalled how his fiancée Honey died in an accident three years ago and he blamed himself because he was driving. Though he was determined never to marry, but now thought to himself, 'If I can get a new close friend then why not a girl of my own?' After his travels, he appreciated the beauty of nature and felt that life may just be worth living.

Tom held Kina's hand and said, 'Whoever brought tears to your eyes is a lucky man. I wish I could have a girl like you in my life.'

They entered the dining hall together and she felt shy because her colleagues were seeing her in a sari for the first time. Dr Leena came up to her and whispered, 'Why not marry him? He is tall and handsome and seems to admire you.'

After the introductions were complete, everyone relaxed and were enjoying themselves, when Dr. Sharma hailed Inder as he was leaving with his family. She turned and their eyes met just like two strangers.

'Meet our guest Dr. Tom Rice the eminent surgeon from New Zealand.'

Inder chatted for a while, but refused a drink and left. The waiter came up to her and told her that someone wanted to meet her on the veranda. She was puzzled, but put her glass down and went outside. It was dark and someone caught her left wrist in a vice. She realized that it must be Inder. 'So the white man is satisfying you now. How hungry are you for kisses?'

As she tried to get free, the grip tightened. He whispered, 'Whatever you do will go against you so keep quiet. Let me satisfy your hunger for kisses so that tonight you won't require him.'

He lifted her face and saw that her face was red and eyes were blazing. He bent down and started kissing her. She struggled for a while, but gave in and was lost in his passion. He then started kissing her like a savage almost bruising her lips and before pushing her aside, slapped her cheek and said, 'I hate you. Cheap woman!' And left. For a while she sat on the chair not knowing what to do. She went to the washroom, and washed her face, applied lipstick to her bruised lips and joined the crowd. The dinner lasted till 11 p.m. and then saying goodbye and reminding Tom of his talk at 8.30 a.m. she left the hotel.

Bhola Ram gave her a note, which she opened: 'I believe the white man is leaving the day after tomorrow. To satisfy you I can keep you as my palace woman. You will earn good money. Inder.'

This was too much and she decided to just keep away from him.

***

Kina and Tom drove up to Narkanda the next day at 11a.m. It was a long drive, but good, and he was fascinated with the high mountains and the slopes which would be ready for skiing soon. He was a keen skier and he admired the slopes. They ate their lunch and drove to Fagu, where there was mist even while the sun was shining. It was late evening when she left him at his hotel. They said goodbye and she left him to rest before his long flight to London.

Now alone, she recalled Inder's note and wondered how anyone could be so cruel to someone he once loved. She realized that Sita Devi was right. It is difficult for a commoner to understand a royal. She must not dream. The story of the poor girl and handsome prince was over. She was able to fall asleep only in the early hours of the morning.

At around 8 a.m., the phone rang. She thought it was the hospital; it was Inder. 'What about coming to my office tonight, since the man has left? The offer of money is not bad, and it will satisfy you,' and the instrument was replaced on other end. How far can one stoop, she thought and renewed her decision to stay away from him.

Chapter 10

THERE WAS A sudden rush of cases with congenital defects from the remote areas around Shimla, and even from further away. It seemed her talk on the local channel worked. Kina was happy because it kept her busy and by the time she went home, she was too tired to think. One day, nanny requested her to buy some items from the Mall. She took the list from her and went with Ramu. She parked the car below the main road and walked to Sahib Singh's store to buy what nanny wanted. She loved this store as it was convenient to buy everything from one place. The owner took the list as the three assistants were busy with other customers. Kina browsed around as he started filling the basket.

Suddenly she saw Ramu walking up to a couple and saying, 'Namaskar Sahib.'

She heard the husky voice say, 'How are you Ramu?'

It was Inder with a girl he called Ashaji. He came near her and told Sahib Singh, 'Please do attend to Ashaji because we are in a hurry.'

The man, who was holding her list smiled, wished him and took a slip of paper from the lady. She observed the woman closely. She was of average height, well groomed in a pink chiffon sari. Though slightly plump, she had a fair, glowing complexion, a broad face with blunt features and slanting brown eyes. She was certainly beautiful. Her head was covered, and the heavy matching jewellery of diamonds and rubies showed she came from a rich, royal family. She pointed to two bottles of perfume and Sahib Singh put them on the counter. He then attended to Inder, who put some of his stuff on the counter. She waited, but lost her temper when Inder asked him for some cuff links and Sahib Singh, ignoring her moved to another counter. A side glance showed that Inder was enjoying seeing her lose patience. His meaningful smile infuriated her.

She picked up the list and interrupted Sahib Singh who was talking to Inder. 'So you serve people based on their status Sahib Singhji?

'Madam your list is long and contains only small cosmetics items. Please bear with me. I will be with you in a minute.'

'Thank you,' she said as she turned to leave the store.

'Please Madam!'

'What a temper. It seems some people are not only rude and brainless, but don't know when and how to talk. I must pity you Sahib Singhji. You should not even entertain such customers in your reputed store. If you continue, people will be too scared to come here and your reputation will be endangered.'

She pretended not to hear, then there was a laugh and a sweet voice saying, 'Inder you're very rude. What is wrong with you?'

She left the store and did not see a bike coming towards her. It bumped into her and she fell and hit her head and left foot. The wounds started bleeding. Darkness enveloped her and the voices around her seemed to come from a great distance. After a while, she recovered took the help of the cyclist and told him not to worry, as it was her fault.

The man said, 'Madam you foot is bleeding. Please let me take you to the hospital.'

'No thank you. I will be fine.'

She look a handkerchief from Ramu and tied her foot but as she bent down again she felt she was fainting. She held on to Ramu's hand, waited a while and walked slowly to a boulder, which she held on to, till the dizziness passed.

A soft voice said, 'Let me help you.'

She didn't reply, and the voice spoke again. She looked up, saw Ashaji and smiled, but then saw the man at her side and her temper rose.

'Thank you,' she said coldly. 'Don't worry, I will be fine.'

She turned to tell Ramu, 'Let's go,' but she passed out.

When Kina opened her eyes she was in the ICU and saw people standing around her but she was blank. It was only on the next day, when she was given her first oral drink that she came to and was told she had suffered a concussion and had a lacerated foot, but that there was no bone injury. She was discharged on the fourth day and advised to rest at home and then attend physiotherapy for a whiplash injury of the neck, for which she had to wear a collar. Though she had recovered, she felt exceedingly week and decided to rest.

***

It was past 4 p.m., when she came out of the theatre and there was a call from casualty. Dr. Sharma was at the other end of the line. 'Dr. Kiran where are you? If you are free can you come to the Chief Casualty Officer's room to see a case?'

She changed and went to the Chief Casualty Officer's room.

Dr. Sharma said, 'Dr. Kiran meet Thakur Inder Singhji and his bhabhi Ashaji.'

The smile vanished from her face as she waited for Dr. Sharma to continue.

'There is a lacerated wound on the left wrist. Though it is not deep, it requires suturing and they wish to get it done by a plastic surgeon.'

She looked at the woman, smiled and said, 'Please lie down on the table and I shall examine you.'

She rang the bell and asked the nurse to get a small sterile tray for a change of dressing. She exposed the wound and left to wash her hands. When she retuned, everything was in place. She examined the wound, which was deep. She cleaned it, applied an antibiotic and put on a fresh dressing. She told Asha that there was nothing to worry about. It could be done the next day under local anaesthesia, in the routine list. 'Just let me know what time suits you,' she added. 'You don't need to fast. How do you feel?'

'Well thank you. It was a nasty knock!'

As she turned to look at Dr. Sharma, Inder asked, 'Who is your other plastic surgeon?'

'What do you mean Sir, I called Dr. Kiran.'

'Please tell me. Patients are allowed to choose their doctors aren't they!'

'Yes Sir.'

'So I want another surgeon.'

'But Dr. Kiran Ö'

'Please no buts Sir.'

'Dr Goyal.'

'Please fix it with him and we will be here tomorrow.'

'He is junior.'

'But he is plastic surgeon. I shall pay madam's fee.'

Kina turned and said, 'Please do as he says Sir. But patients should also realize that though they have the right to choose their doctors, they have no right to waste one doctor's time to examine a patient and then call for another as though they are buying vegetables. I must say that I admire the rich and famous with their show of money; especially the so-called rich and royal. Keep your fee. Give it to a beggar as a token of charity which I doubt you have ever done in your life.' Taking hurried steps, she left the room and banged the door shut.

She was still livid when she returned to the theatre, but when she heard that a burn case was fit for discharge, her anger was forgotten. She was happy that the girl would be going home after months.

She bumped into Dr. Sharma on her way out of the

hospital. 'I am sorry Dr. Kiran but I can't understand why he changed his mind even when the woman insisted she wanted it done by you.'

'Don't worry Sir!' Kina said.

'I must say you really gave it back to him. I saw his bhabhi smile when you told him to give your fee in charity. This is the first time I have seen Thakur Sahib so determined to get his way, even refusing his bhabhi's request.'

As Kina was about to get into her car, the blue Benz stopped near her and Asha Devi emerged from it, calling out her name. Kina stood holding the door and waited.

'I am sorry. At times I don't know what happens to Inder.'

'Don't worry, his fee won't affect the running of my house,' Kina said and winked at her. 'You're funny when you are not angry. You're Kiran to others, but I know you as Kina. Am I right?'

Kina blushed, as Asha Devi continued, 'The man who told me this is stubborn and is acting like a mule, but I fail to understand why!'

'The poor mule is so innocent, and to compare this person to that gentle animal is insulting it. You should rather call him a pig head.'

'Kiran don't.'

'You don't know me. If Dr. Sharma was not there I would have boxed his ear; and I was close enough to him to do so.'

'Really?'

'Yes. Oh there he is, the big mighty man. I am sorry I must leave. I don't ever want to look at him,' Kina said, as she entered the car, closed the door, waved and smiled at Asha Devi. She turned her face away to avoid him and told the driver to take her to the Doordarshan office. She bent her head back and closed her eyes. She felt she was getting tired too frequently and decided to see a doctor.

As the car passed him, she turned her face away. It was enough and he had gone too far in insulting her. He knew she was involved in an accident and he didn't even call to inquire about her. A man who just a few weeks ago had claimed to love her; he was only good for Sita Devi, a dumb, beautiful woman.

***

They finished the audition of her Pahari programme at the Doordarshan recording room, and the team decided to have coffee at Clark's Hotel, insisting she join them. She couldn't refuse when her co-singer also agreed. She told them that she would meet them at the restaurant after calling her registrar. This was her first visit to this famous hotel and she found its location and the view of Shimla from there fascinating. As she stood at the entrance of the restaurant to locate her friends, her eyes met those of Asha Devi, who smiled. She was sitting next to Inder's brother. They resembled each other, except that the brother was slightly plumper and shorter.

She then saw her group and walked over to join them. They were sitting not too far from the royal gathering of two woman and two men. She observed the elderly woman in a beautiful pink sari. She appeared very stately and had an authoritative presence that demanded respect. She must be his mother she thought. Fancy coming to this place only to see these people, but Inder's absence pleased her.

'You seem to be in deep thought Dr. Kiran,' said Sunder, one of the team members from Doordarshan.

'Oh. I was thinking about our future auditions.'

They ordered coffee and light snacks and discussed the summer festival of Shimla.

'You must participate,' Sunder said.

'If you think so,' she replied and looked at the other table by chance. Inder had joined them, their eyes met, but she decided to avoid him.

The next time she accidentally looked at the table, she observed that he was still looking at her. She got nervous and spilt her coffee. As she wiped it, she wondered what to do, and decided to leave, but when she found they were leaving, heaved a sigh of relief. She filled her cup with fresh coffee and was about to take a sip, when a soft push made her spill the coffee again. She looked up and saw that he had deliberately walked past her and pretended to bump into her. She was glad no one at her table noticed anything.

When they left, a waiter at the door gave her an envelope. Kina felt really frustrated. How could she take a path that would not cross his? On the way home she opened the envelope and read:

> You drink coffee like a monkey. Next time wear an apron so you don't spoil your dress. At times I wonder how such an ugly girl was ever touched by me a handsome man. So you also insulted me today. The next time you do so, I shall teach you a lesson.
> Inder.

The phone rang after dinner. Asha Devi was on the line, 'Kiran did you see the Himachali programme on the Shimla channel?'

'No.'

'You were on the show. It was recorded at Village Bani. So Inder was caught red-handed by his mother. You were singing "Uchia Ridia Bansi bajanda ho; Dhangra jo chara dawarju Minjo sade ho". He was wearing a pink turban and sitting on the dais. You were very good. What a melodious voice and those dancing steps! He was also watching the TV, but when his mother turned to tell him that she knew whose gold band he was wearing he had disappeared. We all laughed, when we discovered that he had left the house. Poor Inder. Then when he deliberately made you spill your coffee, my husband said that we must do something for him. He looks restless these days. I think you should make up and then box his ear. So Inder also tried dancing, but I must tell you something. Your pig head is good at the Nati dance of Kinnaur. We will meet in the hospital tomorrow,' she concluded and disconnected.

She wondered what his mother's reaction was, then shrugging her shoulder decided to forget it.

***

It was past 1 p.m. when she left the theatre and entered her office to relax. There was small envelope on the table. She opened it and read:

> So seeing me you got frightened and didn't drink your coffee. Poor hungry girl; like a monkey always craving for food, but scared to spill it. The unisex dress is made just for you, like a uniform for my office cleaners, but it more suitable for a monkey like you.
> Inder.

She recalled how she entered the surgeons lounge for a coffee after a case, but then she saw Inder sitting with Dr. Sharma. She was not in any mood for further comments, so decided to leave when Dr. Sharma called out, 'Dr Kiran come and join us for a cup of coffee.'

'Thank you Sir I shall wait for my registrar,' she smiled.

A sidelong glance showed him looking at her from head to toe. He turned to Dr. Sharma and asked, 'Why do you all wear this unisex dress as though you belong to a green army regiment?'

'Oh no,' Dr Sharma laughed. 'This is theatre dress. It's the same for everyone who works in the theatre and is very convenient.'

'Oh. I didn't know!'

She knew he was deliberately talking to make her look at him and felt happy she was able to ignore. 'Mighty man; I hate him,' she thought and left the lounge.

When she opened her eyes she was still sitting with her legs on the table. She did not know for how long she had slept, but looking at the paper in her hand, she smiled. The frequency of the notes was increasing; it seems the arrogant royal is no longer so angry.

Chapter 11

IT WAS PAST 8 P.M. by the time they completed the surgery on a young man from Rampur. He had fallen off a slope – his right forearm was badly smashed and the skin was completely peeled off, besides fractures in both legs and a blunt injury to the abdomen. Three surgeons worked on him and once it was over, they decided to dine out with their juniors. Dr. Sharma suggested Devico on the Mall, which was close to the hospital. The restaurant was full and while they waited for a table, someone pushed Kina from the back. She was irritated and looked, 'How cheap,' she turned to look at Inder with a frown. He was wearing a dark blue suit with a red striped shirt.

'So the dress has changed,' he whispered looking at her from head to foot. She was angry, and stuck her tongue out at him.

'Monkey,' he said and laughed. Then turning to Dr. Sharma said, 'Thank you for all you did for us. In spite of the angry resentment of one of your colleagues.' He laughed at her red face and winked, 'Well I paid the doctor's fee, Sir.'

'It seems the doctors are hungry!' He looked at Dr. Sharma with a smile.

'Yes. We have had a long day.'

Inder looked at Kina with a sardonic smile, pushed her again and went to a table on the side. She was furious and glared at him, but he ignored her. She saw his mother with

Asha Devi and another very sophisticated elderly woman who appeared to be from a royal family at the table.

The doctors were given a table and they started discussing the outcome of the multiple surgery they had just performed. The waiter brought their food and two additional dishes, which were non-vegetarian.

'We did not order these,' Dr. Sharma said.

'Sir it was ordered by Thakur Sahib and he has also ordered ice-cream.' The waiter said.

Kina knew he was trying to get her angry, but she kept her cool and avoided looking at the other table. They were still eating when the family rose and Asha Devi came to their table. Looking at Dr. Goyal she said, 'All is well doctor and thank you.'

'It is all right Madam it was my job,' said Dr. Goyal as he stood up.

'How are you Kiran?' Asha Devi asked. Kina smiled at her, but the smile vanished when she saw Inder standing behind looking at her with an amused expression.

'I am well thank you,' she responded.

Asha came close to her and whispered in her ear, 'You can really get angry, and stick you tongue out as well.'

Kina blushed and when she looked up he was grinning at her and winked as he turned to go. 'I hate him,' she thought

***

Kina was about to doze off when the phone rang. 'The Rajmata of Chamba saw you today for the first time and she thought that a monkey face is not good for a handsome man like me. She has asked me to reconsider the relationship, which I am doing.'

Kina didn't reply and replaced the instrument. She was angry again.

Suddenly she remembered a small note given by the waiter as they were leaving. She took it out, knowing full well it must be from him.

Everyone at my table noticed how you stuck your tongue out and thought that you were a wild monkey. Somehow I now have an urge to meet you before I take my final decision. I hope the ice-cream has cooled you down.

Inder.

She returned from hospital on a Saturday morning around 11 a.m. and had a sudden desire to take a long-distance drive to forget everything. As she reached home she saw the blue Benz standing at the porch. She felt she couldn't cope with any more stress from anyone in that family and decided to return to hospital but it was too late. Ramu came running out and said, 'Rajmataji is waiting for you!'

Kina thought she must have come from Chamba. Recollecting the phone call the night before, Kina decided to finally end everything. She was nervous, but taking a deep breath, decided to face her to prevent gossip reaching her uncle and aunt in Chamba. As she entered the sitting room she saw it was his mother. She was sitting straight on the sofa reading the morning paper, and looked up when she heard Kina's steps.

'So you were in the hospital, even on a Saturday,' said the woman as she looked at Kina closely from head to toe.

'Just like her son,' Kina thought and kept silent.

'So you're Kiran?'

'Yes!'

'How long have you known my son?'

'Your son?'

'Don't act. Thakur Inder Singh.'

'About a month or so.'

'Are you in love with him?'

Kina didn't reply, but her face went red.

'Sit down and relax, why are you so tense?'

This irritated Kina, and she said. 'I am not tense, and why should you expect me to be so?'

'Tell me frankly about your relationship.'

'What do you mean?'

'How far or deep has it gone?'

'Oh, there is no depth.'

'You just want to enjoy his fame and fortune and to be seen with a handsome man. He is royal and handsome, isn't he?'

This inflamed her. She looked straight at the woman, who had no expression on her face, but was watching her intently.

'There you're wrong. When I first met him, I liked the man, but I did not know who he was. I did not like him because he was handsome, famous, rich, or whatever you think of your son. I have enough of my own and am not interested in the qualities you mentioned. The glamour of someone being royal or rich, has never affected me and will never do so. So please don't think of me in that manner.'

'You're frank when you get angry, aren't you?'

'I am frank whether 1 am angry or not.'

'You do have a temper!'

She did not reply. The woman then asked in a low voice, 'Do you like him or love him?'

Kina maintained her silence.

'Look up woman and answer me.'

'Why should I?' Her face was red as she looked defiantly at the Rajmata.

'Very arrogant and stubborn aren't you?'

'Perhaps it is especially so when I am forced to give a reply to something I don't want to talk about.'

'Really? Even to his mother?'

'Yes!'

There was the sound of footsteps and the door was opened. Nanny with Ramu brought in a tea trolley with snacks. Kina thanked them and told them to leave, as she would serve the Rajmata. The woman refused the snacks and asked only for tea. She made the tea and asked her how much sugar she would like, but turned red, as the latter was observing her closely.

'I take one teaspoon,' she said and took the cup.

Kina put three teaspoons in her own cup.

'Do you always take three teaspoons of sugar?'

'Not always. Only when I get nervous, self-conscious and worked up, especially with elderly people who are slightly stern like you are, asking me so many personal questions. I may even need to take five to stabilize myself. Sweet tea helps me to relax,' Kina said and winked.

'It seems I upset you. '

'Yes! But not as much as I had expected you to.'

'You're funny,' Rajmata said with a soft laugh.

'Am I?'

'Yes. You also have a bad habit of winking. It is not suitable for women to wink.'

Kiran looked at the woman's face and ignoring her remark on her winking said, 'It seems you're rather amused.'

'Very much so. Besides sticking out your tongue, winking is also very amusing.'

'Oh!' Her face turned red.

'Now I know why my son fell in love with you. You're not only different but so open and straightforward. Good looking too, except when you stick your tongue out like a monkey,' the Rajmata said with a laugh.

'Oh did you see me do it?'

'Yes,' she laughed openly.

'Well he does make me angry, and I perform this gesture because I can't hit him.'

'Do you know how to hit a man?'

'Yes. I am an expert, but I am slightly scared to hit him'

'Why?'

'He is clever. He only makes me angry when there are people around and very discreetly too. So what can I say or do?'

'Come and sit near me.'

Placing the cup on the trolley Kina sat next to the Rajmata. The latter took her left hand and asked, 'Where is his ring?'

'Oh, it does not fit me and I took it off because it is so difficult to understand him.'

'Do you mean he is very difficult?'

'Very.'

'Tell me.'

'Well, I didn't know the difference between the expressions "women in the palace" and "palace women" so I spoke casually. He slapped me hard and walked away. I tried to ask him what I had done wrong, but he refused to talk. My friend Dr. Leena told me the difference. I was very disturbed earlier but now I am very angry with him.'

'Why'

'He brought his bhabhi to the hospital, made me examine her, waited quietly till I gave my advice and fixed the time for the surgery, and then to insult me he demanded that my junior should perform the operation. Is that fair?'

'It is not right and I fully agree with you!'

'That is one reason. The other is that he is so unpredictable.'

'Now take out your ring,' the Rajmata said, holding Kina's hand.

She opened her bag and gave her the ring.

The Rajmata slipped the ring on her finger and said, 'Yes! It is loose.'

She then removed a band from her own finger and slipped it on, in front of the other ring.

'There, now it won't slip off.'

'Yes, but it is of no use to me now. You can take your band back.'

'Why?'

'He called up last night to say that he is reconsidering his relationship with me.'

'And you believed him.'

'Why not, he must be repenting giving me his ring.'

The Rajmata laughed and holding her hand, bent down to place a kiss on her forehead. She said, 'You're not only different but you are lovable, my child. Don't take off this ring.'

'Thank you for your affectionate kiss but I shall return it when he asks me to do so. You can't force your son to do something he doesn't want to do. And I would not like to be with a man who does not love me and threatens to reconsider his relationship as though I am a disposable object with no feelings.'

'You're angry with him'

'Yes very much so. I have already told you'

'But can we be friends?'

'Of course!'

'Even if you don't become a member of my family?'

'It hardly matters.'

'But it will hurt.'

'Yes! But that is destiny.'

'You will miss him.'

Kina didn't reply. Then touching her hand said, 'I like you, you're like my mother, who always nagged me because I was tomboyish and wild. But at heart she loves me and wants me to settle down, though I have defied her all these years. Yes! You do remind me of her.'

'Thank you for telling me. But looking at you I am sure you still love him. Am I right Kina?'

She did not reply.

'Look up and answer me!'

'I won't ever again believe in the word "love". I was so carefree in the past and now I am in a mess.'

'You will be happy again my child. I still insist on your wearing that ring with my band.'

She nodded. 'Just to please you till he tells me.'

'All right, and I shall also call you Kina because I do love you my child, and we will be close friends.' The Rajmata said as she rose and planted a kiss on Kina's forehead.

'Thank you.'

'We are leaving for Bharatpur tomorrow and I wish to see you there very soon.'

She then called out, 'Asha come out let us go.'

The surprise on Kina's face made her smile and she said, 'You are lovable, and knowing my son, he is deeply in love with you. Anyway, let us see when you two stop fighting.'

Asha Devi entered the room and put her arms around Kina's waist from the back.

'Wasn't I right when I described her, Mother?'

'Yes. Let us go but take my advice don't take too much sugar,' she turned to Kina with a smile.

Kina nodded and followed them to the car. The woman kissed Kina's forehead again and said, 'I am very happy and satisfied to meet you, my young Kina,' and hugged her before sitting in the car with Asha Devi.

She returned to the house and rang the bell. Looking at nanny she asked, 'Where is Ramu?' 'He is not well. He had a headache and now has fever.'

Kina went to his room. He was lying down with his head covered in a muffler. It looked familiar. She touched his face. He was hot so she gave him a tablet and asked, 'Ramu where did you get this muffler?'

'Madam, Thakur Sahib gave it to me.'

'When?'

'When you were in the hospital in the VIP suite, Sahib booked for you!'

'Tell me in detail.'

'When you had that accident, Sahib rang the police and your car came. He waited till you sat in the car but then suddenly you fainted, so Sahib left Memsahib there and sat next to you as Bhola Ram drove to Snowdown hospital. There he got senior doctors to examine you and stayed there till you were shifted to the special room. He rented the VIP suite and stayed there for the night. The next day you were shifted to the suite. Though there were nurses on duty for 24 hours, Sahib stayed in the room next door, all that day till you came around and opened your eyes.'

'But I never saw him.'

'I think the doctors said that you should have no tension, so he told me to stay with you and let him know. Madam, I don't know her name, came the next morning and made him eat food. He was upset and kept saying, "Oh my God how unaware I was!" Since I was in and out of the hospital, I caught a cold and he gave me his muffler and bought a new sweater for me. He arranged for his driver to get me medicine. He is a very nice man Madam, and now we are close friends. He was very worried about you and even when he went home, I had to ring him every day to keep him informed about your progress.'

'Why didn't you tell me earlier?'

'He told me not to stress you.'

So Inder was there and she thought he didn't care. She remembered Asha Devi saying he was very worried about her. 'Kiran he loves you dearly do just go back to him.'

She decided to call him and looked at the time; it was only 3 p.m. She recalled his mother saying she hoped to see Kina in Bharatpur soon. She decided to meet Inder. She asked Ramu if he knew where he lived.

'Yes. I went with Bahadur to collect Sahib's clothes when he was staying in the hospital with you. It is a beautiful, big, white house with several uniformed guards. Bahadur told me his other house is like the palace of Chamba.'

'Do you know Bahadur's number?

'Yes.'

'You are clever aren't you? Come, call Bahadur and let me talk to him.'

He dialled the number and gave Kina the phone.

'Bahadur this is Kiran. Where is your Sahib?'

'He is in the cantonment Madam. He is playing a polo match. It will be over by 4 p.m.'

'Thank you!'

She went to her room, changed into a dark green woollen Kulu dress with a matching green checked jacket over it, she flung a pashmina shawl over her shoulder and left the cottage. She was now determined to meet him today whatever the outcome. She arrived at the cantonment, parked the car next to the army mess and walked to the shamiana where people were watching the game. She sat just outside the shamiana on a green patch and watched the game.

She tried to identify him, and finally located him in khaki jodhpurs on his white stallion. With the wind blowing through his hair he looked so young and relaxed, and he played well. The game was coming to an end and the men were cheering for the army team to win, till someone said, 'Don't waste your breathe. Can't you see the civilians are winning? They have a wonderful captain in Thakur Inder Singh.'

She thought, 'Why don't I take an interest in the game like his other girls?' She looked around and saw Sita Devi sitting with his mother. She was suddenly depressed and felt giddy. A man sitting near her asked if she was all right. She waited for the giddiness to pass, looked up, smiled and said she was fine. She got up, ran to the car and left the premises. She heard someone calling out, but ignored it.

As she drove she couldn't control her tears. Kina arrived home and went to her room. She lay down, looked at his ring and decided to take it off. As she was about to do so, she recalled her promise at Jot and in Shiva's temple at Hudsar that she would only do so if he told her. Kina just lay in bed thinking about the past month, with no energy to do anything. At around 5 p.m. Nanny told her there was a phone call for her. She picked up the instrument.

'How are you?'

'All right'

'May I come to meet you?'

'Why?'

'Didn't I tell you last night that I am reconsidering our relationship?'

'Oh, yes. Do come.'

'Won't you ask me about my decision?'

'I know! You were with Sita Devi, so there is no need to ask.'

'You're confident.'

'Of course! That is why she didn't threaten me again.'

'Threaten?'

'Leave it be. It is of no consequence.'

'No. Tell me about the threat.'

'Why should I!'

'Anyway now I must retrieve my ring as it is of no use to you!'

'You're very right.'

'So?'

'I will send it to you today if it is very urgent. Ramu knows your house.'

'No. You promised me at Jote when I stopped drinking, that I would take it off your finger myself.'

'So come. Today is Saturday, I am at home.'

'Thank you, but please don't cry. I can't stand tears.'

'Poor man, so many women weeping as he ends relationships. It is so easy isn't it Thakur Sahib? Such an innocent and soft man with a lovable heart who can't stand tears! Don't worry I won't be one of them. And of course, unlike the others, I am just an ordinary woman.'

'Anyway, I am sure you are feeling sad, but what can I do? This is my life.'

'There I agree with you,' she said and replaced the instrument.'

She changed into faded jeans and wore her black polo-neck sweater, tied her hair in a pony tail and put on sport shoes. She decided to return the rings and then go for a long drive alone to cool down and think about her future. The sound of a car brought her to the present. She came out and she saw the ambassador coming up the slope. It seemed his mother had gone. She waited at the staircase near the porch. He had changed into casual clothes. He came up to her and said, 'We must go out to sort this mess!'

'Oh, why not here?'

'I don't know about you but I feel sad about breaking this short relationship at the place where we met so often.

'Very sentimental man!'

'I am, don't you know me?'

'Not till today!'

'Why don't you look at me Kina?'

'Don't take my name.'

'Touchy,' he said, 'you look very depressed, but I did request you not cry!'

'Stop it. Let us just go for a short drive to end this drama,' she said in dry cold voice. 'You're dragging it too far.'

'All right if you say so! Where shall we go? This must be your choice because it will be our last meeting.'

'Just down the slope'

'In my car, if you wish!'

'All right come.'

He opened the door for her, she sat in the car and he took the drivers seat. He reversed and drove down the slope.

'Stop here as it reaches the middle of the path. Now take off your ring along with the band your mother put on this morning to hold it in place, because as such it is not meant for me.'

He took her hand in his, raised it, looked at the ring and started touching it. Kina turned her face away and waited. Realizing that he was doing nothing, she looked at him angrily and said, 'Please take it off and give it to your wife.'

'But who is that woman?'

'I shall take it off myself, throw it in your face and walk out.'

'You will Kina?'

'Yes, I will.'

'Oh how angry you get! But at this moment I do love you.'

He held her in his arms and started kissing her. She struggled but the hold tightened and she started responding. Suddenly she recalled the incident at the cantonment, and like a wounded animal she pushed him away and said, 'Please don't play with me. I am sick of your drama.' She opened the door to leave, when he held her back and slapped her cheek.

'How dare you!' Kina was livid.

'I do dare. I am sick of your behaviour and tantrums Kina even when I love you.

'I don't love you now.'

'Tell me the reason.'

'I went to the cantonment this afternoon and saw Sita Devi!'

'So you thought. I was back with her? Tell me Kina! Is this your trust in me? Look into my eyes.'

She did and was lost.

'Talk,' he ordered.

'I am sorry!'

'Remember I only love you. There is no one else, but darling please try to more careful not to make me angry and slap you! I shall love you till Ö'

She put her hand on his mouth to stop him.

'I am sorry to tease you for so long and to upset you.'

'You do slap very hard. It hurts.'

'I am sorry,' and he kissed her cheek, touched it gently, smiled and asked, 'Better now?'

She nodded. He held her in his arms and kissed her again. She put her arms around him and responded; and they were lost in each other. The sound of a horn made them part.

Inder looked at his watch. It was past 7 p.m. 'Oh, my I have to be with my parents. They are leaving early tomorrow at 4 a.m. Never mind I can't leave you now. Hungry?'

'Yes.'

'Let's go to the Cecil,' he said, then looking at her clothes, said, 'I am getting used to this uniform.' He held her again and continued, 'I must get married within the next few days as mother suggested. It is getting too difficult for me to resist you and stay in control.'

He started the car.

'What about your going home?'

He laughed, 'Ma, will know where and with whom I am; to patch up.'

'Your mother came to see me'

'I know.'

'What did she tell you?'

'She said, "Son, Kiran is an uncut diamond. She is priceless. She is not beautiful but very attractive and lovable. So go get her back within the next few days, and never try to polish her. She will always be yours and today I realized how lucky you are to find her from nowhere."'

'What was your reaction?'

'I said I knew that, and that I loved you dearly. I would never be able to live without you. Happy?'

'Yes!'

'I shall give you food if you promise never to doubt me again.

'I do.'

He bent down without a care kissed her cheek. 'It looks like Kina is in love! And hungry too,' and laughed.

They sat in the private dinning room, at the Cecil, where the table was set for two.

'Don't you feel embarrassed bringing me here in these clothes? They are most unsuitable for dinner.'

'Why should I? You wore them to annoy me but they are the same clothes that brought us together the first time. However, what you wore when you came to the polo match was beautiful.'

'You saw me?'

'Yes but you ran away. I called out to you, but like my monkey, you were too quick to catch. I shall always remember my mother's words. She was so excited after meeting you and told me Kiran is my young friend. Whatever you do or wear, I will always be in love with you my Kina,' and he kissed her.

'It has been almost a year since I played at the cantonment. I have been so engrossed in that woman's affair.'

Inder started narrating the harrowing time the family had undergone:

> The case was held in camera as requested by us to protect the family's reputation from the public eye. Our advocate was Mr. Ghosh from Delhi and hers was P. Khanna from Jaipur. First came the divorce case. It was argued for two days.
>
> Her advocate claimed that my brother was cruel to his young son. That he left both of them, to live with Asha Devi at Rampur. However she, being a devoted wife stayed on at Bharatpur with her son waiting for her husband to return.
>
> Then Mr. Ghosh came up with evidence of how she tricked Yuvraj into marrying him, when she was four months pregnant. He showed the records of the gynaecologist whom she had asked to terminate the pregnancy; and the date of birth of the child and proved that he was a full-term baby. He presented pictures of her at parties and of her friend Ravinder Kumar, with evidence of his being her boyfriend even after her marriage. He placed the records of the two abortions at Jaipur in front of the judge. The DNA test results showing that the child's DNA matched Ravinder's were also presented. Finally, he described the evidence to prove she was poisoning my brother with cyanide and rat poison, which was why the family kept him away from her. The divorced was granted and she was sentenced to five years imprisonment for attempt to murder.
>
> She was a real actress and fainted but nothing was found wrong with her.

Next came my case. The file was opened and closed because she had been proved to be pregnant, and was blackmailing me with the help of the police inspector. Then again the cook and the man who sold the cyanide powder were punished.

Ravinder, I think is still in love with her and asked for the child's custody. We agreed so he took the boy. He refused money and told my mother he would marry her when she came out of jail.

So after a long while, my family was relaxed. All these days the family was very busy and so was I, but I did miss you! My mother saw your programme at Bani village and told me the next day to marry you as soon as possible.

They were both silent for a while. 'Tell me about the threat,' he said.

'Leave it.'

'Please darling.'

'Sita Devi told me on the day I came to Chamba from Hudsar that if I come between the two of you she would teach me a lesson. But then nothing happened.'

'I will tell you why. When she came to Shimla, she asked me to dine with her. I told her I was busy. That evening as I was getting ready to leave the office, she entered. It was very unusual for a woman from such a respectable family. I entertained her with a cup of coffee, and she started crying, telling me how much she was in love with me. Well, you know I can't stand tears, so I went up to her and started consoling her! She said that since she had been with me for a long time, she was sure I would marry her. I realized then that the Rajmata had not told her about our conversation, and that surprised me. I told her that I was already engaged to you and that I would be marrying you soon. So everything was cleared and we parted.'

'Why do you make me angry?'

'I shall not now, as it will affect your health, even though

I love to see you angry. That is why I stayed away from you for so long. I had a tough time in the hospital, being so close to you and yet told not to cause any stress. Let us finish dinner or do you wish to stay in the hotel where I kissed you madly?'

'You were horrible.'

'Yes! I am a very jealous man. I wrote nasty notes to you. I offered you money. Nasty man! I was exceedingly upset to hear about the episode of the snake and was just too jealous darling. Now let us finish, I must meet Ma. She will not sleep till she hears what has happened between us.

Chapter 12

KINA LEFT THE theatre at 11 a.m. and went to her office to relax. When the phone rang, she picked it up. It was Inder.

'Where are you?'

'At the hospital.'

'What about lunch?'

'I have to attend a recording at the Shimla TV Channel at 2 p.m.'

'So there is no time for me.'

'Please, Inder,' she pleaded, but the phone went dead. She called but was told he was busy in a meeting. She left a message that she would join him at 2.45 p.m. as she was free at the hospital that day. She waited for some response, but there was none.

She arrived at the recording studio with ten minutes to spare. She wore a navy blue Gujari dress and heavy silver jewellery, as traditional in Chamba state. She was accompanied by Sunil and the other girls. The theme was based on an army man and his beloved who was adamant that he build a house on the mountain for her if he wanted her to live with him. Though he started by offering her a balu (nose ring), jewellery for forehead and saris, she remained adamant. Then she started singing a song and danced to the song of the mountain.

Main tanio basna, main tanio rehna.
(I will only live with you)

Pahara wich Bangloo pawa oh faugia . . . Pahara. . . .

(If you build a house on the mountain, army man).

Jania na chhadhi kari oh mani gori oh mani cchori balu Gadhai dingo oh meri chhoria.

(Please don't leave me young maiden I shall buy you a nose ring).

Na jana deni, ghare basani oh meri goria.

(I will not leave you but make you my wife, I shall give you a nose ring).

Pahara vich bangloo pawa de chhonia . . . pahara. . . .

Sari leaydingo o h meri gori . . . oh. . . .

Na jana deni, ghare basani pahara wich banglo pawa oh faugia.

Mian tion basna, tian Rehna pahara wich bangloo pawa de faugia.

She was so engrossed in the recording that she didn't notice someone entering the room. After the recording was completed, she spoke briefly to the assistants and went to a side room to remove her jewellery. She then decided to ring Inder and be with him. 'He is getting too possessive,' she thought and smiled. No more fights now. As she emerged from the room, she saw Inder talking to the Director near his car. She went up to them, and the Director, Mr. Sood, smiled and said, 'I must congratulate you for the beautiful alliance, but Sir,' he turned to Inder, 'do allow our artist to sing for the people of this state occasionally.'

Inder laughed, held her hand and said, 'I shall never interfere. That is my promise.'

He shook hands with the Director and led her to his car. She looked around for her car.

'I have sent both drivers off. Any objections?'

'No. When did you come?'

'So you wish to have a house on the mountain before settling down with me?'

'Oh you!'

'You were beautiful and I wonder about your talents besides the one which can ignite a fire and I do love it.'

There was silence for a while as he drove, till they exited the studio gates.

'Hungry?' he asked.

'Yes!'

'Always hungry my Kina.'

'Where are we going?'

'To see our future home, then to the one where I live, and about which you have never asked. The girls I met and who became my friends were all rich. Yet they were so interested in the grandeur of my life and my home in Shimla, but you have never even bothered to ask about these.'

They drove along the Shimla-Rampur road and after about four kilometres he turned off the main road. It was a narrow, steep climb up a slope with tall pine trees on both sides. They reached the hill top and he stopped the car in front of a gate on which was a board saying 'Bharatpur House'. The guards opened the gate and he drove down a road lined with sprawling lawns, edged with flowerbeds. On the flattened hilltop was a double-storeyed, white house overlooking Shimla on all sides, against the background of snow-clad mountains in the north-west. Inder stopped the car under a covered porch in front of a wide staircase leading to a covered veranda.

A fleet of servants wearing grey uniforms and green turbans were waiting for him. A tall man in a white uniform with a green silk turban opened the car door. Inder gave him the keys and opened the door for Kina. He held her hand and whispered, 'Welcome to our future home. I wish I could kiss you, but there are too many people around. This is the only disadvantage of living in this house.'

They entered the veranda and the main door into the house. Kina saw a spectacular layout. The central hall had a majestic staircases covered with red carpet leading to the upper storey. She looked at the grandeur of the spacious hall with a beautiful central chandelier, and oak furniture, covered in blue and red velvet tapestry, the thick Persian carpets on the floor and expensive antique pieces arranged on small tables. However, it was the bay windows, with their thick lace and red velvet curtains drawn that attracted her attention. She walked up to the central window and was lost in the view it presented.

A soft cough brought her back to the present. She turned and saw him looking at her with a peculiar expression on his face.

'Have I done something wrong again?'

'Yes. Only the hills, snow and the beauty of nature appear to attract you. Tribal girl. All my girls, though they were royal, loved the grandeur of the house.

She came close to him and said, 'But you are wrong. More than nature, I love you, never forget that Inder you are my love and will be till I die.'

She was in his arms. 'Oh why do I love you so much my wild monkey? Do you like this house?'

'It is beautiful, but it's too grand to live in. I am not used to it. I wonder how many times I shall annoy you because I am too simple.'

He didn't reply and started kissing her.

'Can I go up?'

'No. The suite is mine and will be yours after our wedding.' Now listen to me carefully. The threat to you was taken seriously by my mother, so we are going to Bharatpur tomorrow.'

'Why?'

'You ask her. I believe you're her young friend.'

Kina glanced around the hall and wondered how she would be able to adjust to this grandeur.

'Don't worry my love, I shall always be with you. I did not visit this house after the incident in Musoorie. It was under government protection. I always stayed in my official residence. This was opened when mother discovered that her younger son was in love and planned to settle down. So she started giving a new touch to this house. Let us go. We have to be at the cottage where they are waiting for lunch. We will stay there tonight. Surprised?' 'Yes.'

'Well, we are on our way to Bharatpur to marry.'

'But Ö'

'Leave all to mother. Everything has been arranged between both sets of parents.'

***

They got into Inder's official ambassador with Bahadur driving at 6 a.m. the next morning.

'Take the Hindusant-Tibet road via Narkanda.' Inder told Bahadur. He then rested his head against the back of the seat and closed his eyes. There was complete silence. Kina looked out of the window. The sky was clear with a few white clouds. The road ran between mountains of dense forests one side and a deep gorge on the other side with grassy green slopes and wild thorny foliage. The tinkle of the flowing hill stream lulled her into a dream state.

Kina glanced at Inder. He appeared deep in thought and there was no expression on his face. 'Poor Inder,' she thought, 'how much he suffered, and that too when he was so young at heart, yearning to enjoy his career and love.' She felt an urge to see this woman, who for years made his life miserable, denying him the right to visit his own beloved birth land. Then she thought of how she must be suffering in prison without her son. Kina decided to leave it to the man up in the sky and forget the past. She realized that Inder was sleeping she too dozed off, but a touch awakened her. She looked at him questioningly.

'I didn't sleep last night. The past was haunting me. The reply to my question of why I had to suffer, despite being innocent, came to me early this morning. It was written by God in my destiny.'

He turned suddenly to the window and holding her hand said, 'Look Kina.' He pointed at the beautiful valley lying between the tall cedars and pines on the hills surrounding it. 'There is Naldehra. We will soon reach Narkanda.'

The spectacular views of the Himalayan peaks including the mountains of the Pir Panjal, as always enchanted her. He pointed to the ski slopes and the narrow trekking paths and said that the view from the top of the mountain was even more majestic. 'You can see the hills and the valleys all around and about two kilometres from the top of the peak is the open grazing ground called Jot-Bagh.'

'Have you been there?'

'Yes for skiing and I also visited a fort built by the Gurkhas called Hatu Peak, it is eight kilometres from Narkanda. The Gurkhas invaded this place in the nineteenth century. I stayed there for a week in early March and really enjoyed it.

She smiled at him and said, 'Really? What a nice way of enjoying a trip.'

He laughed, 'None of my girls were tough enough or loved nature like you to come with me to this heavenly place. We will eat at Kumar Sain village about 17 kilometres from here on the way to Rampur,' and holding her hand said, 'how enjoyable it is to travel with someone you're in love with.'

The car slowed down and Bahadur said, 'Sir Kumar Sain is only a kilometre away and this is the best place for you to eat, but you decide.'

'This is perfect,' Inder said.

He turned to Kina and said, 'This area is surrounded by apple orchards. The hub is to the north of Narkanda, in Thanadher and Kotgarh where an American married a local girl and started the first apple plantations.'

'Yes I know. He was Samuel Evans Stokes. The family still lives in the same village which also has the temple of Koreshwar Mahadeva.'

They ate lunch under the trees and then Inder took Kina

to the edge of the mountain and showed her a temple of Lord Shiva on the slopes below. 'We will not go there today because time is running out. But on the way back I shall take Mrs. Inder Singh there for his blessings.'

They returned to the car and proceeded on their journey. As they drove through the town she saw a young boy playing the flute she nudged him and asked, 'Can I buy one?'

'You play Kina?'

'Yes.'

'All right.' He asked the driver to stop the car and the boy came up to it. She got down, selected one and said, 'Let me try it before I pay you.'

Kina played a stanza of a song, nodded, paid the boy and touching his shoulder gently, thanked him. As she turned to the car, she saw that Inder had taken their photographs.

The road to Rampur now descended steeply towards the Sutlej river. Inder started telling her about Rampur. 'It was once a large state and included Kinnaur. It was ruled by the Bushaur dynasty, but was later split into smaller states. Our Bharatpur state constitutes a part of the lower Kinnaur valley and a part of Rampur state. My father and his elder sister Bimla Bua married in the capital city of Rampur. I still dread her. When we were young she was very bossy. We tried to stay away from her and she resented that. We called her horrible Buaji and I named her white Bhalu but my parents found out, and I was warned. Her visits became more frequent after she lost her husband. She only wore white saris after she became a widow. She loved Yuvraj because he would say yes to everything, but resented me and complained about me. I hope she won't be there. Even though she is old now, she is still aggressive.'

Inder laughed and asked her to play the flute for him. 'I want to discover all your talents,' he said.

Kina played a few stanzas of a Shimla song and stopped.

'It is beautiful and you're good. Why don't you sing a song?' Inder asked her.

'No, not now.'

'All right, we are close to Rampur. The city is located at a lower level on the banks of the river Sutlej. It is cool in the early mornings and the evenings, but warm in the afternoon. The city has several temples such as that of Raghunath and Narsinghji but there is also a Buddhist temple there. Every year during the first week of November, they have a fair and sell dried fruits and beautiful woollen items such as shawls. People come from all over Kinnaur. Villages are scattered between apple orchards and the snowy mountains are a beautiful backdrop.'

They bypassed the city and turned left. Inder told her that they would soon enter Bharatpur state, which was 30 kilometres from Rampur but at a higher attitude. 'It is spread over the north-east part of lower Kinnaur and part of Bushauar. Unlike Kinnaur it has very grassy green, deep valleys, natural lakes, lush green pastures and fascinating meadows. There are mountains all around, but they are not barren as in upper Kinnaur. They are green and you can see the snow-clad mountains of Zanskar, the greater Himalayas and the Dhauladhar ranges in the north-east.'

As he spoke, Kina looked at him. He was so relaxed, enjoying himself, talking to her about his beloved land. She didn't interrupt him, and he continued. 'We have a semitropical and alpine climate here. We believe in the goddesses Durga and Kali, and in Lord Shiva, and there are some Buddhist shrines as well. Though the state is small it was never invaded, and the people live in peace. They are mainly shepherds and Gujjars who rear their cattle. The local traders deal in apples, dried fruit and wool. The tribal women are beautiful, like you Kina.'

The climb became steeper as they arrived at an opening between two hills. He said it was called 'khirki', a window to view the panorama of the city on the other side. The capital city was Maithli. He told Bahadur to stop and holding her hand took her through the gap and told her to close her eyes. He guided her along a few steps and told her to open her eyes. She saw the beautiful layout of the city, nestling in the deep green valley surrounded by high mountains. The view took her breath away and she was lost to the world. The sound of a camera clicking, as Inder took her picture, brought her back. He then asked Bahadur to take a picture of the two of them together and held her, even though she protested and felt shy.

He looked at the watch and said, 'We must leave it is 5.20 p.m.'

As she turned, he whispered, 'This may be our last chance before the wedding,' and putting his arms around her kissed her lips. He then continued, 'Behave; you will be viewed through microscopic eyes inside the palace,' and laughed.

The road turned to the right and encircled a grassy green slope covered with tall pine trees. She then noticed the Bharatpur flag flying on both sides of the car bonnet. They drove down the road encircling the city in the centre of the mountain slopes. Kina saw some people returning home with their flocks of sheep and cattle. Some were walking and others were on cycles and small vehicles.

Kina observed how everyone gave right of way to the white car with the green flags and red lion in the centre, the insignia of the erstwhile royal state. They stood with folded hands as the car went by. Inder opened the window and accepted their greetings with folded hands. She saw smiles on the faces of those people – so simple yet so affectionate. Even though they were no longer considered as royalty, yet their people still had great regard for them. Kina wondered why. She had observed the same attitude at the Chamba club when Sita Devi entered the room.

The car turned to the right and after a short drive stopped in front of a large wooden gate. The gate was opened by guards wearing the same uniform she had seen in his house at Shimla, and they saluted as the car passed through the gate.

The road was now beautifully well maintained, and Inder told her, 'We are arriving at the palace now, and you will be under the control of my family.' He winked and continued, 'Kina darling, please try to be a bit diplomatic and not don't show your boredom as you did at the Chamba club.'

The car approached the flattened part of the hill, open on all sides and she could see the yellow palace on the elevated mound, the royal flag of Bharatpur flying with the mountains in the background. 'What a beautiful place,' Kina thought.

Inder tried to cover her head with a scarf, and told her to wrap her shawl around her. He gave Bahadur the flute. 'Keep it with you and put it into Madam's luggage. But be discreet and make sure no one sees.'

'Yes Sir,' the driver replied with a smile.

The car was now in the palace grounds, covered with sprawling lawns and flowers of different types and colours. Then she saw a fountain of white marble and a statue of a woman in a sari with a beautiful figure pouring water from a pitcher into a pond full of lotuses of different colour. The car stopped in front of a wide staircase under a covered porch.

Several people had assembled there, and most of them were in the same uniform. Inder told her to adjust her scarf. The car door was opened by a tall, middle-aged man who saluted Inder as he came out.

'How are you Ram Singh?' he said.

'Well, your highness,' and then wiped his eyes.

Inder touched his shoulder and said, 'I am here and happy.'

The gesture touched Kina and she got her answer to why the people still adore these old rulers. They have a sense of humanity with a personal touch, which was lacking in the politicians of today. The erstwhile rulers still talked to their people in their language and tried to understand their feelings. He nodded with a smile to the retinue of servants, shook hands with them and then opened the door for Kina.

He whispered, 'Come Kina we are home.' He waited for her to emerge, and did not hold her hand as he used to. As they took the first step on the carpeted staircase there was a sudden beating of drums and the Bharatpur anthem was played by the royal band. They stood at attention and when the band stopped playing they took their next steps up the long staircase. Children sprinkled rose water and rose petals on them, till they arrived at the veranda. She saw his parents standing there with his older brother and sister-in-law on either side.

They bent to touch his parents' feet and they blessed them. His mother held a silver puja tray in her hands and performed the ritual welcome puja. She first applied a tilak on her son's forehead and then on Kina's and blessed them. Inder then went up to his father and they embraced. The latter's face was red, but he kept his emotions under control. She recalled her father saying that blue blood can always be judged by their emotional control. The family members hugged him one by one and then his mother held Kina's hand and said, 'Welcome to your home Kina.'

The Raja Sahib turned and walked with his sons on either side into the house through the huge, beautifully carved wooden door with silver latches. The ladies followed. They entered a small corridor and Asha Devi took her hand, 'Come we will go to the sitting room. Let the family be together. It is an emotional moment, especially for his father. They will then make their offering as they had promised, to the family deity, as thanksgiving for his safe return to this house. After that, they will join us.'

Kina nodded and they entered the sitting room. It was more expensively decorated than the Shimla palace with old oak furniture, heavy velvet drapes and thick Persian carpets. There was a fire in the grate and the portrait above it was striking. The royal couple were in their official attire and looked so young.

She looked out of the bay window and holding Asha's hand said, 'Come and look at the sunset. God is going to his abode but is taking a last peep from behind the mountain, spreading that purple hue all around.'

Asha said, 'You do love nature, and are so simple. But don't forget Inder, he should be your first love.'

Kina smiled and said, 'Yes he will always be my first love,' and winked.

'Kina,' she heard a voice say, 'women don't wink.' She looked up to see Savitri Devi standing with her husband and sons.

'Come and sit,' Inder's father spoke with a voice of authority. Kina sat next to his mother.

'So you're Kiran. I am told I have to call you Kina.'

He was tall and fair with a serious look on his face that had no expression and his brown eyes looked at her just as Inder did.

'Yes!'

'What is the meaning of this name?'

'I don't know. My name is Kiran, but I am called Kina at home.'

'I knew your grandfather, Thakur Shamsher Singh. Once I was in Chamba to attend a wedding in the palace. I went to his beautiful house on the corner of the mound overlooking the river and the valley, with the backdrop of the snow-clad Dhauladhars, the palace and the chaugan.'

'I was born in that house.'

'Why when your parents lived in Dalhousie?'

'They lived in Dalhousie, but Chamba is my birthplace. My grandfather was very fond of me, so he often took me to Chamba, even if it was against my parents' wishes. I spent my childhood and teens with him and was more at home there than in Dalhousie.'

'He travelled a great deal and put in tremendous hard work for the development of the state,' Inder's father said.

'Yes and I often accompanied him. That is how I fell in love with nature and the simple people who lived there. I learnt their folk tales, songs and their religious beliefs. I must have travelled to every nook and corner of the state with my grandfather.'

'You're a surgeon?'

'Yes by accident.'

'Why?'

'I wanted to be a historian, but someone told my grandfather that I cut and sew with both hands so I could be a good surgeon. He insisted and now I like surgery.'

'What sort of surgery do you perform?'

'I correct defects to beautify people.'

'Do you know how to ride?'

'Yes and drive as well. I started riding as a young child, though I can't say how good I am.'

'Your mother is well but she has been told not to travel. I spoke to your father.'

'Thank you for telling me.'

'Tell me, which car would you like to drive now?'

'I drive a Toyota and am very happy with it. I don't want any other car.'

'So your parents are not attending this wedding?' Bimla Bhua asked.

'No they are not!'

'What sort of wedding is this Bhai Sahib and what is the urgency?' She said looking at her brother, who didn't reply!

'Devinder tell me,' she was angry.

'We will talk about it later,' he replied in a grim voice.

'I am not happy.' The voice was cold.

The tea trolley was brought in and everyone was quiet while the bearer served the tea and snacks. Inder sat without an expression on his face, till his brother touched his shoulder and he nodded and smiled. The bearer came up to Kina and asked how much sugar she would like.

'Four cubes Ram Dev for madam,' Savitri Devi said. Kina looked at her and smiled.

'How do you know Savitri?' Her husband asked her.

'Well, Kina takes sugar to calm herself, when we oldies

try to interrogate her.'

'Oh! I am sorry Kina.'

'Don't be. Sweet tea relaxes me. Rajmata warned me not to wink at you, because according to her women don't wink.'

'But you wink?'

'Yes.'

This time he laughed openly and said, 'I am very happy to meet you and talk to you my girl.'

He rose after drinking his tea and told Asha to show her around the palace. He caught hold of Inder's hand and left the room. Somehow she felt Inder was slightly upset. There was silence in the room after they left.

Bimla then said, 'I must talk to my brother about this unusual alliance.'

The woman waited then said, 'I am talking to you Savitri.'

Kina saw that her mother-in-law was feeling uncomfortable.

'You fixed the marriage and did not inform me. I found out from the Rajmata of Chamba. You even forgot to show me the sari and jewellery your future daughter-in-law would be wearing. Am I not you elder sister-in-law?'

'The dress Kina will wear is not one that the brides of Bhartpur wear. It has been designed by Inder and he also selected the jewellery. So what can I do?'

'Well even though you have picked a girl who is not royal, our brides always wed in a sari. I must clear this with my brother.'

'Please Buaji, let your brother be happy after so many years.'

'Don't tell me what to do,' and the woman left the room.

The room was silent again and Kina was embarrassed. She rose and asked Asha Devi if she could go to her room to relax as she was tired.

She smiled at her future mother-in-law and said, 'Don't worry. My grandfather used to say that the fresh breeze of the morning blows away the problems of the day before.'

The woman smiled back and said, 'My Kina is a fresh breeze

for all of us. Asha, take her to her room. She can see the palace at another time.'

Suddenly Kina realized that she was tired. They walked to Inder Bhawan, which was open and under Ram Singh's control. He led them to the sitting room. The dÈcor was mainly turquoise blue and white, with a deep blue carpet. The bay windows were closed and draped with lace curtain, though the thick velvet curtains were drawn apart. The modern black and beige leather sofa set was arranged around the room and a fire was burning in the grate. The grandeur was similar to the main palace and over the fireplace was a painting of Inder as a young man standing in the indigenous royal dress holding a jewelled sword. His eyes and smile were mischievous. She recalled his mother saying that he was clever; after teasing the girls, he would bribe them to avoid being reported. He was smart and handsome and had several girlfriends.

Asha devi broke her reverie and said. 'Let us leave. I brought you here just to give you a glimpse of the wing. The other side where you will stay is always reserved for very important guests.' She smiled and whispered, 'Mother does not trust Inder, so she told me to keep you away from him till the wedding. According to our custom the bride and groom don't meet before the wedding. But who can trust Inder?' she laughed.

They left the wing, and Asha pointed to the top of the central staircase. 'That is his room upstairs and will soon be yours after the wedding. The only gloom has been caused by Buaji, and I feel sorry for her. We all respect her, but at times she must understand that she is rather old now. She wanted Sita Devi to marry Inder and is furious about the rejection and about not being consulted. She must be arguing with her brother at present, but she is wasting her time. Father wants Inder to be happy after the ordeal he went through.'

Her room was between the main palace and Yuvraj's wing,

opening out on to a square terrace garden with a view of the mountains in the north-east. 'It is called the pink bedroom.'

The entire dècor here was pink and white, and each room in the wing had a different colour scheme.

They sat on the sofa and Kina said, 'Tell me about your life with Yuvrajji.'

Asha smiled and holding Kina's hand started talking.

I lost my parents in an accident when I was two years. My uncle the Raja of Kinnaur brought me up with his son who was one year at the time, as his own daughter. They spoilt me and to start with I was arrogant. I studied at Tara Hall in Shimla when I saw these two Yuvrajs at the Cecil Hotel. One was quiet and the other naughty, always looking at girls. During my graduation year I met Yuvraj at the cantonment while 1 was out riding and he had came to play polo. We fell in love and he promised to marry me. That was why he decided not to study further. But Inder wanted to become a bureaucrat. There was a very close bond between the brothers. Inder was young, over-protected and innocent. Yuvraj worried about him in spite of his being good in his studies, and an excellent rider and polo and tennis player.

We were officially engaged and I noticed that Yuvraj made frequent trips to Jaipur. About a month later, he told me Inder had fallen in love with a girl who was looting him, making him drink and study less. He sent his spy to make inquiries and discovered that she was known as a bad character. Thus to dissuade this relationship he approached her. Inder saw this and avoided her. He went back to his studies for the IAS Examination.

Yuvraj thought this was the end, but the girl was clever. We were just about to marry when he told me about an FIR lodged against Inder at Mussoorie. The entire family was in a dilemma. The girl was ready to take back the FIR if one of the brothers married her. Inder was posted in New Zealand and to save him Yuvraj got married.

I was heartbroken, but we decided to be together and married secretly in a temple. I stayed with my uncle who knew the truth and on Yuvraj's behest, decided to wait.

The woman was evil but she was shocked when he refused any physical relationship after the marriage. He warned her that should she ever talk, he would expose her pregnancy. After the marriage he took her to a, doctor who declared, in writing that she was almost five months pregnant when she married him and blamed Inder. He allowed her to stay in the same suite as we now do, gave her money, and permitted drinking parties with her boyfriends from Shimla and Jaipur, mostly army officers.

When the boy was born and her parents celebrated at Jaipur, he told her that he was filing for a divorce. She was shocked and started staying away from Bharatpur.

In the meanwhile Raja Sahib had a mild heart attack but Inder was not informed as he recovered very swiftly. When the boy was three, he was put into a convent in Simla. Then Yuvraj started complaining of pain in the stomach whenever he ate at Bharatpur. This alarmed us and we caught the cook whom she had brought from Shimla.

Then the family, except Inder, were told of our secret court marriage, which had taken place in Mumbai. We had a son while Yuvraj stayed at Kinnaur in hiding, trying to collect all the evidence against this woman. Inder's friend helped and everything was proved in the court where the case was conducted in camera.

'How old is your son?'

'Thakur Binder Singh will be one year old next month. Inder found out all this from his mother in Shimla, when I joined the family. He cried and both brothers hugged each other. Then you had the accident and he was so worried that his mother decided he must now settle down with you. The Rajmata of Chamba who came to Shimla with Sita Devi, was informed. She agreed that the marriage should take place at the earliest, as after your trip with him to Hudsar, the state is full of gossip. My mother-in-law went to Chandigarh and met your parents. They agreed, so this wedding was fixed in a hurry.'

A maid entered the room and said that the Rajmata wanted to see Asha. When Asha returned she found Kina asleep. She covered her with a blanket and awakened her only at dinner time.

Chapter 13

A GENTLE KNOCK, the sound of the door opening and the fresh, cool breeze awakened her, but she lay still, wrapping the quilt around her more snugly. She realized that a maid had entered when she heard the sound of anklets. She was aware of the soft clink of china, as the tea tray was placed on the table, the stirring of the fire in the grate and drawing of the thick curtains at the windows. The sun came streaming in and she sat up in bed. The maid came up to her and touched her feet. With a smile, she said in a soft voice, 'I am Bindu the daughter of Chhote Sahib's nanny! He asked me to serve you with fresh tea and biscuits.' The girl then gave her a white envelope marked Inder Bhawan. She opened the envelope, took out the scented paper and read: 'You must eat something even though it is not allowed. But the ritual will take a long time and food will be served late. I do miss you! Bindu is to be our maid in Shimla, Inder.'

She took a cup of tea with a biscuit from the girl, who started pressing her legs gently. Bindu was of medium height, with a broad face typical of a hill maiden, with blunt features, a fair complexion with slanted eyes. She wore the traditional Bharatpur costume of a loose green kurta over a knee-high ghagra. Her head was covered with a red and green woollen scarf tied back with a knot. Beautiful, heavy silver and multicoloured beaded necklaces adorned her neck and she wore a gold nose ring.

Kina asked her, 'Do you always wear this costume?'

'Yes.'

'It is beautiful.'

'That is the reason why sahib ordered three costumes for you. But they were of expensive pashmina wool, including a scarf. Instead of the ghagra, he ordered tight churidar pyjamas. He even bought silver jewellery for you. However, he told my husband, Banwari, to keep it a secret, and told me that my Chhoti Rani was half tribal. He asked me what I thought of you and I said that though you were not as beautiful as Rheena Yuvraj, you were attractive and different from the royals. He laughed and told me he loves you very much. Chhote Sahib would get into trouble and I would lie for him. He was very naughty, and teased the young girls working in the palace, breaking their pitchers or firing his airgun to frighten them. He was always in trouble with Rajmataji but Raja Sahib loved him very much and spoilt him. Maharaj has not laughed as he did yesterday, for a long time. He was worried about Chhote Sahib.'

'What about Buaji?' Kina asked.

She laughed. 'They have a love-hate relationship. When he was young he would steal her puja money and disturb her while she prayed. She was always complaining about him to Rajmataji. Then the very next moment, they were together just like the night before at dinner. She saw your wedding dress and jewellery and laughed and hugged him, saying you would be the best wife for him.'

It was getting late so the girl hurried to collect the tray and leave. 'I must leave before anyone sees me. Rani Sahiba you're supposed to be fasting.'

Kina lay back and thought of the dinner last night. She was late coming down, but they waited for her. They were all dressed for dinner. The men were in their simple indigenous woollen kurtas and tight pyjamas wearing the traditional Bharatpur shoes. The ladies were in their best attire. Kina had worn a simple black dress with red Kashmiri embroidery. When Inder entered with Buaji, everyone smiled and it was a happy family that sat down for dinner that night. She observed the Raja's look when Inder refused a drink. He was holding a glass of apple juice in his hand and when he looked at her and nodded, it reminded her of the trip to Jot.

They laughed when she told them that she had sold her white Morris to four medical students and was shocked the next time she saw it – it was painted red, green and yellow. She noticed that Inder did not speak to Asha.

Just then, Asha entered the bedroom and asked her to see her wedding dress. She laughed and said, 'We are not on talking terms at present, and he must be even more grumpy now because he had to wake up at 5 a.m. for the oil ceremony.'

Kina looked at the dress and smiled as she recalled the event at village Bani. It was a grassy green, expensive, Pashmina kurta. The embroidery was the same indigenous work that was on the dress given to her by the Gujjars, but it had the tight pyjamas of the Gaddi women instead of loose salwar of the Gujjars. There was a matching woollen scarf. She looked at the jewellery. It was gold instead of silver but copied so well by the jewellers that she thought it was from Bharatpur.

'This dress was sent by your uncle from Chamba.' Asha said. 'Inder ordered it in Chamba and requested your uncle to send it.'

She then gave Kina an envelope with a letter from her uncle. 'Did I not tell you on your return from Hudsar Kina? And the dream has become a reality. When he sent the bag for you, he sent me a letter, where Mian Sahib wrote of his love for you. He asked me to order the dress and keep it a secret. Your aunt was furious with me when she learnt of the wedding and the reception at Chandigarh later this month. What a romantic tour it must have been – love on the road to Hudsar. Do accept our wedding present Kina Thakur, we love you.'

She looked up with tear-filled eyes. Asha came up to her and said, 'Tears are not good in the eyes of a bride who is so dearly loved by the groom and all of us. Now get ready by 7 a.m.'

***

The old Raj Darbar was the venue of the small wedding ceremony, as desired by the groom. It was 7.45 a.m. when the bride was led into the hall. She looked at the mandap, the priest and the small gathering. The local music played on drums, pipes, flutes and the conch reminded her of the temple at Hudsar, where everything was ready for their marriage. Inder's mother gave her a special garland of gold coins and told her to put it around Inder's neck. She looked at him in his royal attire, the same as in the painting she had seen in Inder Bhavan. He was wearing a cream silk turban with expensive white pearls hanging on either side of his face. Then she saw the feather held by a diamond broach in the centre of the turban, a long pearl necklace around his neck a white zari achkan and bare feet. He put a similar necklace around her neck while looking down at her with a smile.

They were made to sit in front of the mandap and the pandit, while the parents sat on either side of them. The Hindu ritual was complete after the couple took seven rounds of the sacred fire and were pronounced husband and wife according to Hindu law. The priest was asked to take them to the local family deity in one of the rooms of the palace, where they made their offerings. They then went to the main temple of Goddess Kali on the mountain; it was past 10 a.m. by then.

The couple still held the red silk rope knotted in the centre which was to be opened in front of the deity according to the royal family's traditions. They sat at the back of the white Benz, driven by Bahadur and with Asha in front. They were quiet as the car turned to the right and drove up the steep hill. It was a clear day but the sunrays were finding it difficult to penetrate the tall trees of the Bhairon jungle, where it was claimed that several people had actually seen the deity's vehicle, the lion, at night.

'This is a reserved forest and no one is permitted to hunt here. It is still under our royal domain,' Asha said. Turning to Inder she continued, 'You're very quiet. Why not tell Kina about the legend.'

He didn't reply and she smiled, 'Still angry? But why? It is the Hindu custom not to see the bride in her dress before the wedding; it is considered inauspicious.'

Inder laughed. 'I am not angry.'

'You better not be, because I know many secrets about you.' And Asha Devi narrated the legend.

Inder's great-great-grandfather was the chief of a local tribe, the Khalasis, who were renowned as the hunting devotees of Ma Bhagwati and their staunch believe in sati and female infanticide. They used to sacrifice a female child to Devi, but when the British stopped the custom, goats were used. Inder's ancestor was in the forest hunting and he arrived at the top of the mountain alone. His name was Dharinder Singh. He was tired and slept under a tree. A hissing sound awakened him, but he lay still as he saw two white snakes. After a while they went down the slope. He threw a coin on the area where he saw the snakes and heard a strange sound, as though it had hit a metal pot. He waited till his men joined him and then spoke to his Rajguru. He was advised to perform a yagaya and pray for one week. After that he was supposed to wait and see if he had a dream or an event occurred to instruct him to touch the pot. The night after the yagaya, Goddess Kali came to him in a dream and ordered him to dig out the pot. She told him, 'The money in the pot will help to build a temple and expand your local rule. But underneath the pot is a smaller one. Keep it with you and open it only after the temple is built. Then take it out and place me in the centre of the temple on a pedestal. Don't remove the handles of the pot. They will be the site for the nags to sit and pray for me. Always offer them milk and never hurt them.'

The temple priest always keeps two pots of milk on either side of the deity for the nags to drink. That is how this temple was built, and over time became known as our royal temple where no one else can pray except our old tribe the Khalasi.

The deity brought luck to this family and more when an English officer was saved by Inder's grandfather, Devi Singh. He was given the title of Raja. That was when the state changed from being a simple Zamindar's land to a royal one. Bhawani Bhawan, the palace was built and a wing was attached with the birth of each son. The family found mines for the precious stone neelam (blue stone). They became rich and came close to the British.

They reached the top of the mountain and the car stopped at one side of the flattened hill. The couple was received by his parents and brother and then taken to the central deity Bhairon, made of black stone, so beautifully carved. They were asked to close their eyes while the priest recited Sanskrit shlokas. Next they climbed up to a covered veranda and a small temple open on all sides. There was only place for the central deity here, even though it was small.

Inder whispered to Kina, 'It is made of seven metals called the seven dhatus.' They were made to sit while the puja was conducted, after which a coconut was broken, the pandit untied the knot that still bound them and blessed them. They were given prashad of puri and halwa – the first food Kina had after the morning tea. It started raining and there was laughter because that meant that the Goddess had blessed the couple. Inder's mother and father came up to them and blessed them. They were followed by Yuvraj and Asha Devi. Kina saw tears in Inder's eyes as he hugged his brother and bhabhi.

As they entered the car, Kina found her eyes filling with tears. Inder's mother came up to the open window and said, 'No tears Kina. We shall soon be together again. Now look after this naughty husband of yours,' and laughed.

As the car drove down the slope, Inder said, 'Bahadur take the Shimla Rohru highway to Hati Koti, to the cottage.'

'Yes sir,' he said and drove down to Rampur Bushar. There was silence for some time in the car. Inder then smiled at her and asked, 'And how is Mrs Thakur Inder Singh?'

'What shall I say?' She smiled back.

'We are driving to Hati Koti. It is a valley of stone temples. It is said that they were built between the sixth and ninth century AD in the Gupta period. It is surrounded by hills and paddy fields, and is situated on the right bank of the Pabhar river. At Hati Koti there is the sangam of three water streams: Bish kuti, Ravti and Pabhar, and is a place of pilgrimage. There is the famous ancient Mata Hateshwari for Ma Durga, and the temple complex also has a temple of Shiva. However the main idol is from the Bronze Age. It has a soft, ethereal glow. It depicts the eight-armed goddess Hateshwari riding a lion as she drives her spear through the demon Mahishasura. My parents wish to go there tomorrow to give offerings to Ma to thank her for returning happiness to the family. I bought the cottage on the slope hidden by tall trees from a Gurkha last year as his had father died and he didn't wish to live in India any longer. Your love for nature is like mine, but I did not know about it at the time. Just one look at this small wood and stone cottage, and I fell in love with it. I renovated it with Bahadur's help. He spent many long hours here to get it done. And now that we are married, I want to spend our wedding night there.'

***

The chirping of the birds and the sunlight peeping though the thick curtains awakened Kina. She could hear a flute playing a Pahari tune. She recalled the drive up the slope on a steep, narrow road. 'The Hati Koti ridge is about 8,000 feet above sea level. It is easy to walk up to it if you're an enthusiastic trekker,' Inder had told her. 'And it is only eight kilometres from Narkanda. Above the cottage are the grassy green pastures where the nomad Gujjar tribes live in temporary shelters with their cattle and above that is the temple of Mata Hateshwari.'

The car stopped in front of the small wood and brick hut with a slate roof and chimney. It looked like a diamond on a black rug. Holding her hand he led her inside the beautifully furnished, vintage hut. It was warm with the fire lit in the grate and windows covered by thick velvet curtains. It appeared almost isolated from the dangerous surroundings of the night that were dreaded by everyone.

They sat next to the fire after they changed from their wedding clothes. He held her in his arms, stroking her hair, while he spoke. She had entered a fairyland, listening to her beloved speaking. She was tired, and lying in his arm under the warmth of the fire, she went into a deep sleep.

She rose and looked around for Inder. She found him lying on the sofa next to the fire, fast asleep. She went up to him and stroked his curly hair softly. He opened his eyes looked at her, smiled and with a glint in his eyes said, 'So Kina is up. Come and look at nature in all its glory'

He took her to the window and drew the curtains. She remained silent, and he asked her, 'Tell me darling, what is the matter?'

She put her arms around his neck and whispered, 'All this can wait. From now onwards Kina will dream and love Inder first, because he is and will always at the top of her heart till her last breath.'

She hid her head against his chest. He held her tight and whispered, 'So my Kina has suddenly matured and loves me above everything else, just as I do her? Yes everything else can wait but not our love on the first day of our wedding.'

He started kissing her and they were lost in each other. As their passion rose, he took her gently to the bed, and knowing that this was true love she was lost in the arms of her beloved. Kina the girl so wild, yet so loveable, suddenly became so wise, and gave way to a passion equal to his, forgetting the physical world around them.